MOROCCAN MYSTERY

MOROCCAN MYSTERY

✦

The Passport Series

Nancy V. Riley

iUniverse, Inc.
New York Lincoln Shanghai

MOROCCAN MYSTERY
The Passport Series

Copyright © 2008 by Nancy V. Riley

All rights reserved. No part of this book may be used or reproduced by any means, graphic, electronic, or mechanical, including photocopying, recording, taping or by any information storage retrieval system without the written permission of the publisher except in the case of brief quotations embodied in critical articles and reviews.

iUniverse books may be ordered through booksellers or by contacting:

iUniverse
2021 Pine Lake Road, Suite 100
Lincoln, NE 68512
www.iuniverse.com
1-800-Authors (1-800-288-4677)

Because of the dynamic nature of the Internet, any Web addresses or links contained in this book may have changed since publication and may no longer be valid.

This is a work of fiction. All of the characters, names, incidents, organizations, and dialogue in this novel are either the products of the author's imagination or are used fictitiously.

ISBN: 978-0-595-48696-0 (pbk)
ISBN: 978-0-595-60793-8 (ebk)

Printed in the United States of America

A very special thanks to my niece, Christyna Vieira da Rosa, for her support, encouragement and many improvements to this text.

And to Erin and Lizzie, thank you for helping me picture it all!

This book is for Aili, Julia and Tom, who shared with me an exciting and wonderful Moroccan adventure.

1

Aili

I had just turned the page in my current murder mystery when the phone started to ring. Now, don't get me wrong, the phone rings a lot, and today *seemed* like any other day the phone might ring. So, naturally, I ignored it. It kept ringing, but I wasn't about to just stand up and leave when the main character's life was on the line! I was beginning to get irritated, and after five more rings, I finally threw down my book and stomped to the phone.

"Hello?" I asked, sounding kind of annoyed.

"Yes, is Mr. Turner there?" an official sounding voice asked, "This is the White House. President Bullard wishes to speak to him." My stomach flip-flopped. A call from the *White House?* I ran into Dad's study, skidding on the polished hard wood floor, my heart thumping. *A call from the White House!*

"Dad! It's for you. It's the White House! I think they said President Bullard wants to speak to you!"

I handed the phone to my father and waited anxiously to hear what was going on. I knew my Dad had been friends with the President when they had been together in business school, and I vaguely knew that my Dad had done some important work on the President's campaign last year. But to get a phone call at *home* from the President of the United States? Now *that* was pretty exciting.

I leaned against a bookshelf trying to look casual, as I listened to my Dad's end of the conversation with the President of the United States. But with a wave of Dad's hand, I was booted from the small office. *Like that will help!* I thought, standing just outside the sturdy oak door. Listening to the conversation, I thought it was cool that instead of calling his old friend by his nickname, "Jed", Dad called him "Mr. President" and "Sir", just like in the movies. "A sign of respect for the man and for the office," Dad had said when I had asked him about it before.

"What's going on?" asked my 11-year-old sister Julia as she came out of the kitchen and saw me leaning against the wall outside the study.

"Shhh!" I shot back, a little sharply, enjoying knowing something Julia didn't, "and turn that stupid thing off!" I pointed to the tape recorder Julia was carrying. Always coming up with creative ideas, Julia's latest project was to go around recording what she thought were interesting and different sounds: the scrape of our dog Bailey's toe nails on the wooden floor, the creak of the front door as it opened, the rustling of the leaves on the orange tree. Her idea was to make some kind of video using cranked up versions of these recordings as interesting sound effects. Julia had over 40 sounds already, and I had had to suffer through my sister's constant "shhhh's" and "quiet's" as she tried to make new recordings. I tried to cooperate with her, but had to draw the line somewhere. Like yesterday, when Julia shoved the microphone against my cheek, trying to get the sound of me chewing gum. I only gave her the tiniest shove, but got in trouble anyway. Sometimes I think it's cool that Julia is so creative, and even tell my friends about her energetic schemes, but I have to keep my pride, and would never tell her that to her face.

"Just tell me why you are spying on Daddy!" Julia whispered loudly.

"Later," I hissed, pushing Julia out of the way.

"What*ever*," Julia said. She hovered in the hall for about a minute, but when her eye caught sight of a hummingbird flitting around a flower outside, she scurried off to try to make a recording.

I was relieved to know more about the phone call than my nosy little sister. Even as a 13-year-old eighth grader, I always feel like my sixth grade sister seemed to find out all the gossip before me.

"I am very honored, Mr. President," Dad was saying, "It would be a great privilege for me to serve you and our country."

Someone said something on the other end of the conversation.

"No, that won't be a problem. Yes. I will do my utmost to serve with distinction. Thank you again, Mr. President. Yes, I will, of course. And please give my best to Sherri. Good-bye."

I didn't have time to duck out of the way before Dad came out of the door. I had never seen his hands shake so much as when he reached down to touch my shoulder. In what came out as almost a whisper he said, "Well, guess what, Aili! You are looking at the next United States Ambassador to Morocco!"

Later that night at the dinner table, we were still chatting excitedly about the important phone call and all that it meant when Julia, who had been uncharacteristically quiet for a few minutes, suddenly paused with a forkful of spaghetti in mid-air and said, "Daddy, I don't think I even know what an ambassador does!"

"Julia!" I turned to my sister, shaking my head in a condescending way, "How do you not know that?" I looked at my parents, quite knowingly so that they could see how smart I was.

"So tell me, Miss Smarty Pants," Julia challenged, "what *does* an ambassador do?"

All eyes turned to me. Darn. What *was* an ambassador anyway? I'm known as the "bookworm" of the Turner household. I always have a book with me wherever I go: in the car, at the table, watching TV, (even in the bathroom!) I read everything: from short stories and romantic novels to true adventures and histories. Really, I'll read anything I can get my hands on. And, because I read so much, I always feel pretty well informed, and love to show off my *ah-mazing* knowledge. Especially in front of Julia.

"Um, well it's … It's well, it's hard to explain in simple words …" I knew my only chance was to try and squirm out of it.

"Well, then use *complicated* words," Julia countered. Julia isn't as book-smart as me, but she is also very bright. And, she does not like me always trying to make her look stupid.

"It's just. Well … er … well, it's just that I don't think I could explain it as well as Daddy." I felt my face glow warm, and concentrated on using my fork to pick at my now-cold spaghetti.

I could feel Dad looking at me and so I glanced up hopefully. Dad was 46 years old, and very fit; he worked out several times a week. He had a kind face, his hair dark brown with only a few flecks of gray in it, and laugh lines on his cheeks, tan from his weekend golf games. He had a great sense of humor, and both Julia and I adored him.

"The Ambassador is the personal representative of the President of the United States in a foreign country," Dad said, "He is the one who tries to give a good picture of America to the foreign country and its people."

"So it's like advertising and PR?" I asked eagerly. I'm interested in all sorts of creative fields, and advertising and public relations were at the top of the list.

"Well yes, it is partly public relations," Dad explained, "He or she also helps American companies doing business in the foreign country and, of course, helps Americans living or traveling in that country. It's also his job to know about the country and how it affects American interests. President Bullard has asked me to be his representative in Morocco."

"Monaco?" Julia asked, thinking about the small country near France.

"No, not Monaco, Julia. Morocco: M-O-R-O-C-C-O. It's a country in North Africa."

"Africa ..." Julia repeated with a sigh, as my own head filled with images of giraffes and elephants. I had been fascinated with animals and the fight to preserve endangered species ever since a fifth grade outing to the fabulous San Francisco Zoo. Snow leopards were a special favorite of mine. Only 2 feet high, they have beautiful, thick white fur with ringed spots of black on brown. But there could be as few as 3,500 of them left in the *whole world* because people hunt them to use their bones and other parts in traditional "medicine". Yuk!

"Yes, but *North* Africa," answered Dad, as if reading my mind, "Not the Africa of the herds of animals and jungles. That part of Africa is further south. Morocco is in the part of Africa where Arabs and Berbers live. Where there are great deserts and high mountains. Lots of palm trees and camels, but no lions and rhinos!"

"H-A-I-T!" Julia exclaimed.

"H-A-I-T!" Dad agreed, laughing to himself.

Ever since she was a little girl, Julia had come up with special words that were her own. It all started with her word for jelly. Because she was only two at the time, she had trouble asking for the jelly. Instead, she would just point and say "lilli". She used it so much, that all of us started saying "lilli" for jelly. As she grew older, Julia came up with more special words, and most recently she came up with just saying letters for sentences. Like "R-A" for "right away" and "O-M-M" when she needed "one more minute" to finish up what she was doing. Her latest letter combination was H-A-I-T, which could mean either "how awesome is this" or "how awesome is that". Plus, it could be pronounced like a word instead of a letter combo.

"So, Dad … will you have to travel a lot to Morocco?" I asked. The thought of having Dad away for long business trips suddenly began to worry me.

"Well, actually, Julia and Aili," Dad paused and looked at my Mom, Nancy. Mom smiled at him and he continued, "Actually, this job means we will ALL be moving to Morocco, and we will live there for at least two years, maybe more. The Ambassador *lives* in the country where he is assigned."

I stopped eating and looked from Dad, to Julia to Mom and finally back to Dad, in shock.

"Move? What do you mean move?" I screamed, "Move away from Palo Alto, our house, our *friends?*" I could not believe what I had just heard.

Julia also chimed in, "We have to move? This is *so* not OK!"

We looked questioningly at Mom and Dad.

"Dad?" I attempted to get some sort of explanation.

"Well, yes, we would all move to Rabat, the capital of Morocco. We will have a big house and you will a have a new school and new friends and …"

"No!" Julia and I cried out together. Tears welled up in my eyes as I tried to understand what was happening.

Mom, who had been quietly watching the discussion now joined in.

"Girls," she said soothingly, "think of the fun this will be! You both love to travel and have adventures, and now you will have lots of both! I know how hard it is to think about leaving Palo Alto, but this is such a great opportunity, for Daddy, of course, but really for all of us."

Mom, a year younger than Dad, had grown up in her father's native Brazil, but had her Finnish mother's blonde hair and green eyes. Living overseas was not something she was afraid of. Instead, she was looking forward to it.

Mom reached out and touched Julia's and my hands with her own.

"It's a big step, I know," she continued softly, "but I also know that the two of you will love it."

Dad could see that Julia and I were still concerned. "I want you both to know," he said gently, "that I would never do anything I thought would be unfair to you. Trust me on this, girls. It will be the experience of a lifetime."

I wasn't sure. Nope, not sure at all.

After dinner, Julia and I sat on the comfy couch in the TV room, trying to watch our favorite show, a rerun of "Full House". The TV room was one of the coziest rooms in the house. Against one of the room's windows was a soft, slightly worn sofa covered in a pink and white striped fabric. Bookcases lined the walls of the room and three of them were reserved just for Julia's and my books. The bottom shelves still had some of our first books, including the much loved (and now very tattered) copies of "Goodnight Moon" and "Pat the Bunny". The higher the shelf, the higher the age range of the book. The top shelves held the books we were currently reading, such as the "Gossip Girl" books and "Catcher in the Rye".

I sat with one of the sofa pillows on my lap, staring at the TV, but there was no way I could concentrate. I was still trying to digest the cold sticky spaghetti along with the fact that our family was going to move to Morocco. Sure, I love to travel almost as much as my mother ("it's in our blood" Mom always said), and at age thirteen I had already visited twenty-eight countries. But traveling to a place for a few weeks and living there were two very different things. I didn't like this. Not at all. Not one teensy, tiny little bitty bit.

"Well," Julia looked up at me. I didn't move, didn't even bother to look her way. "I guess we're moving to Morocco. I mean, maybe it won't be so bad, Aili. A Moroccan adventure for the Turner family. It could be kind of fun." Julia smiled hesitantly.

Julia was always trying to make the best of things. Obviously she would get into bad moods sometimes and make a fuss if things didn't go her way, but in general, she was able to make things work out for the better. Her golden hair and bright smile were all part of her sunny disposition.

I take things much more to heart. I'm cool and calm most of the time, but when I got upset, it is deep and lasting. This was one of those times.

"*Fun*? You think it will be *fun* to leave all your friends? And leave your school?" I demanded, "Your idea of *fun* is to go to some strange country where we know nobody, into a strange house, to a country where they don't even speak English? Sure, it's great for Mom and Dad, but what about for *us*? They can't just mess up our lives this way! They just can't!"

With that, I stormed out of the TV room, passing Mom and Dad who were standing in the hall. Mom looked at Dad and was about to go after me when Julia ran in and stopped her.

"Don't worry, Mom and Dad, I'll talk to her," said Julia, "You know I know how to handle her!"

"H-A-I-T," I could hear Mom whisper to Dad as Julia caught up to me put her arm around her big sis.

"Yeah," Dad agreed, "how *adorable* is that!"

2

Julia

The next day, Aili stayed in her room for most of the morning, still upset at the thought of having to move to
Morocco. Even our dog, Bailey, wasn't able to cheer her up.
But, good old loyal Bailey stayed by her side, and every once in
a while looked up at her and wagged his tail.

"We won't be moving for at least a few months," I said, trying to find the words to comfort my sister. I was sitting on my
bed painting Aili's nails.

"Give me your other hand." I shook a bottle of Hard Candy
hot pink nail polish and started to apply it. "It really will be ok.
It could even be …"

"But what about here? Our home? Our friends? We just say
goodbye to all that?" Aili blew on her nails and wiped away a
smudge I had missed. "What about our dog?"

"Well, Mom and Dad said Bailey's going to stay with Uncle Eric in Mendocino. You know he loves it up there. Plenty of room to run around, no traffic. And we're going to live in a giant house in Morocco and have servants! Real servants, Aili! I heard Mom say so."

"Well, I want to stay here. And I want my friends here! I don't want to leave. No way I am going! No Way! I like it here!" Aili wailed, flopping back on the bed.

I looked around the room and understood how Aili was feeling. The morning sunlight poured in through the windows, making our lavender and white room sparkle. I loved lavender, and it was everywhere. I thought back to that Saturday last summer when Mom and I had painted the room together. I had seen this striped pattern in a magazine and convinced her to let me repaint the whole room in big, broad stripes. We had to move all the furniture and put tape everywhere, first painting the room white and then adding lavender stripes after the white paint had dried. My best friend Talia said it looked like a circus tent, but I loved it. The bed sheets, duvet covers, desk blotters, lamps, picture frames, vases—they were all lavender. The mirror over our dressing table was topped by a lavender bow. Even the lotion had a lavender cap on it. Through the windows I could see the orange trees that shaded the side garden where Bailey's doghouse was. Aili and I had shared this bedroom in our hundred-year old home all our lives, and I suddenly realized that leaving this familiar room and all the memories that lived in it was going to be hard.

"It's not like we won't be back, you know," I said, a new quiver in my voice as I tried to convince myself as I comforted Aili, "Palo Alto will still be our hometown ... it's just like we're going for a really long trip. And I'll bet a lot of our friends will want to visit us!"

I watched as Aili shifted a bit in the bed. "And," I continued, more confident, "I heard Mom and Dad talking ... Marrakech, one of the oldest cities in Morocco, has great shopping, and we would have the first look at all the new styles coming out of Europe ..."

I knew that Aili loved shopping and loved being the first at school wearing a new fashion. She would often sort through Mom's old clothes that were kept hanging in the basement and alter them to fit her and to give them a new twist. She would wear them to school, reviving old styles from the 80's and 90's. Last month she started a new trend—she cut the feet off of different colored tights (neon green, watermelon pink, lemon yellow) and wore them layered, so that a little bit of each color showed.

"Well, maybe it wouldn't be so bad for a while," Aili conceded. She sat up, brightening at the thought of shopping.

"Of course not! We are going to have so much fun!"

Aili sat up and gave me a hug. As we held each other tightly, I thought about Aili. We were alike in many ways. Both of us had blonde hair inherited from our mother and brown eyes from our father. Aili's long hair was usually twisted at the back of her head, held by a clip. I wore my shoulder length hair pulled into a ponytail, having finally decided to grow out the bangs I had had since second grade. Since we both spent a lot of time outside playing sports and riding our bikes, our hair was streaked with golden highlights. A peek into our closets revealed our love for Abercrombie & Fitch, H&M, and Hollister. Aili's outfit today was a pair of jeans with brown ribbed v-necked tee shirt worn over a white tank top. A small beaded black necklace adorned her throat and her ever-present Tiffany heart bracelet (a present from our grandmother on her 13th birthday) dangled from her wrist. Two silver rings, one on her right index finger and one on her left middle finger, were almost never taken off. She glanced at my outfit. White capris and a striped turquoise and white top …

"Hey!" Aili said as she pushed me out of the hug, "That's my top!"

"It is?" I blushed, "Oh, sorry, are you sure?"

"You know it is! And you took it on purpose!"

"You always take my things too, you know. So this is pay-back, Fat Face." I knew my nickname for Aili only infuriated her even more.

"DON'T call me that!" she shouted, "And take off the top now! Right now! Mom!!"

I got up from where I had been sitting and sighed, "Well, I guess things are back to normal! At least maybe in Morocco we won't have to share a room!"

"That will be a relief!" Aili breathed, "I can hardly wait to go!"

3

Aili

I peered out of the window of seat 3A on Royal Air Maroc flight 960 from Paris, France to Casablanca, Morocco. Since leaving San Francisco almost sixteen hours ago, I had watched three movies, had one dinner (gag) and two breakfasts, and had read two books and five magazines. We had landed briefly in Paris, just to change planes. The next leg was to Casablanca, Morocco. Although not the capital of Morocco, it's the country's largest city and where most of the flights from overseas arrive. Now, as we approached Mohammed V Airport in Casablanca, I could make out the first hints of the land below. The plane descended and I began to see the outline of the coast, and then fields and scattered villages.

This is kind of exciting, I thought. *We're in Africa!* I looked over to Julia, still fast asleep in the seat next to mine.

It was now late April, and so much had happened in the past four months, all leading up to this minute, I mused to myself as I stared out the window. A few weeks after the phone call from the President, the FBI investigated Dad to make sure he was not hiding anything about his personal or business life that could cause problems for him or for the United States. Then, there were the meetings in Washington D.C. before the Foreign Relations Committee of the United States Senate. I remembered being overwhelmed by the great halls of Congress and listening intently as the Senators questioned Dad about his ability to represent the U.S. Then, the great day came when the Senate confirmed Dad's nomination and he was sworn in as the U.S. Ambassador to Morocco. Dad now officially worked for the United States Department of State, or "State Department" as people called it, and his boss was the Secretary of State. A few weeks after being sworn-in, we were all on the airplane, bound for Rabat, the capital of Morocco.

The flight attendant came by interrupting my thoughts, gently woke Julia, and asked us to raise our seats in preparation for landing. A few minutes later, the jumbo jet eased down the runway and taxied to the gate. As we stepped off the jetway, into the VIP arrival lounge, we were met by an official greeting party from the Embassy.

"Welcome, Mr. Ambassador and Mrs. Turner, and Aili and Julia. Welcome to Morocco, 'The Land of the Setting Sun' as Moroccans call it. My name is Wayne Plant, and I am the DCM, or Deputy Chief of Mission, at the Embassy."

"Thank you, Wayne," said Dad as he shook his hand, "We are honored to be here!"

We also shook hands with Mr. Plant. Mom reminded us that the DCM was the #2 person at the Embassy (the Ambassador is the #1 person). In fact, when the Ambassador is out of the country, the DCM is in charge of the Embassy and is known as the "chargé d'affaires" (which is French for "in charge of business").

Wayne was tall, about forty years old, but with a boyish face. I liked how his eyes twinkled when he smiled. Wayne had been with the State Department for almost twenty years, and had served in Kenya, France and Jamaica, among other places.

I looked around the crowded VIP lounge. "There are so many people here!"

In fact, many of the senior staff from the Embassy had come to meet their new boss, the Ambassador, and his family, and there were also officials from the Moroccan government and lots of newspaper reporters and photographers. Camera flashes went off every few seconds so Julia and I felt like we were actresses at a glamorous Hollywood premier.

"We're famous!" I grinned as a photographer took yet another picture of us.

"Mr. Ambassador," Wayne said to Dad, "I know there are a lot of people here, but it is customary for you and your family to shake hands with everyone. And, in Morocco, when you enter a room you always start greeting people from the right to left."

We moved to the right side of the room.

"Mr. Ambassador, you should shake everyone's hand. Mrs. Turner and girls, you should shake hands with the Americans and with the Moroccan men. Some of the Moroccan women will kiss you, and you should do the same."

"Kiss them? But we don't even know them!" I exclaimed and gave Julia a wide-eyed look that meant 'Oh, no!'

"Yes, Aili," Wayne answered, smiling, "You just give them two kisses, one on each side of the cheek. You can also say *Met-*

char feen which means 'happy to meet you' in Moroccan Arabic."

Oh, kiss on each side of the cheek, I thought. That was cool, and also seemed sort of Hollywood-ish, plus not so ... weird.

We went around the room (starting from the right, of course) and greeted everyone, and when we finished Wayne said, "If you are ready, Mr. Ambassador, please follow me. You have already been cleared through passport control and customs and your luggage has been loaded into the car."

"Wow," I whispered to Julia, "we don't even need to wait for our stuff at baggage claim! Someone got our luggage for us!"

I looked down at my new diplomatic passport, which was black instead of the normal blue. The diplomatic passport, given to people (and their families) who work for U.S. Embassies around the world, gives them some special rights and also lets them go through special immigration lines when they arrive in a foreign country.

I looked up from my new passport when I felt Julia's hand grab my shoulder. "Look at *that* guy!" she whispered to me.

I followed her gaze to a man in a black suit, with a huge long scar down the left side his face. I quickly looked down, but when I looked up again, he was staring right at us. His eyes were dark, almost black, and unblinking, like a falcon's. I was sort of hypnotized by them for a minute.

"Aili! Don't stare!"

I looked away, embarrassed by my sister.

Suddenly and with a great flurry, we were whisked through the airport, surrounded by security guards and other officials, toward the waiting Cadillac limousine. The American flag was flying proudly from the right side of the car and the State Department flag from the left side. Just like in the movies! For security reasons, the ambassador was assigned a white SUV as a lead car, and another SUV as a follow car. *Quite a motorcade,* I thought, as other passengers at the airport turned to see what the big commotion was all about. *I could get used to this,* and I slid into the awesome plush seat of the Cadillac.

"We really *are* like movie stars!" Julia whispered excitedly into my ear.

"Next stop, Rabat, the capital of Morocco!" Wayne announced.

I tapped on the Cadillac's windows. Thunk. They were thick and solid. Wayne smiled "Armored. The car is armored so it is protected from bullets." My mouth and eyes opened wide, my mind racing, wondering why we needed that kind of protection. Wayne saw that I was nervous. "It really is a matter of general security, offered to all Ambassadors. But Morocco is a very safe country, and you will see, when you go out, or your mother goes out, there is no security detail, no armored car, no need for any of it."

I relaxed, feeling safe again, and started to enjoy the whole spectacle of our motorcade pulling away from the curb. But as I looked back at the airport to see the crowd of people waving goodbye, I saw two men talking secretively and quickly back and forth. As they spoke, one of them turned and pointed directly to our car—it was the scary man with the jagged scar and the falcon eyes.

4

Julia

The limousine sped down the highway toward Rabat, past farms and small villages, past date palms and olive trees growing among ancient ruins. To the west, the Atlantic Ocean sparkled in the sunshine. Little whirlwinds picked up the dusty soil and scattered it in random piles. I stared dreamily out the window, wondering what my life was going to be like in this new and strange country.

"There are about 30 million people living in Morocco. It is about the same size and has the same population as California!" Aili announced, reading from her guidebook, "Most of the people speak Arabic. But it's not the same Arabic they speak in Saudi Arabia. The pronunciation is different and some of the words are different. Many of the people also speak another language, called *Berber*."

I looked over at Aili, sighed out loud, and then turned my gaze back to the scenery outside. *Ber-ber, Bor-ing,* I thought. Where are all the cool animals and bustling marketplaces?

"Ummm … let's see," Aili continued, unfazed by my little display, "*Shokran* means 'thank you' in Arabic and *Manzakin* means 'how are you' in Berber."

"*Shokran* for not reading any more out of that book, Aili! Can't you stop reading for even one minute?"

"Sorry I want to learn about our new country, Julia. I just happen to be interested," Aili apologized sarcastically.

"That's wonderful, Aili," Dad said hoping to head off a quarrel between his girls, "Did you know that many Moroccans also speak French? Since Mommy and I already speak French, we are going to be taking Arabic lessons, and if you like, you girls can take lessons too."

I was concentrating on some of the highway signs (written in both Arabic (all squiggly lines and curlicues) and French) trying to figure out which Arabic letter corresponded to which Western alphabet letter, when I overheard Mr. Plant say to Daddy,

"Yes, Moroccan seaports are very busy, but unfortunately not everything passing through them is legal. It is a very serious problem, Mr. Ambassador, one on which we are working very closely with the Moroccan government. The smuggling is of illegal goods, drugs and even people. Sometimes young children are smuggled overseas to be maids and servants."

Wayne noticed that I seemed concerned, "But it's nothing for you to worry about, Julia and Aili. The Moroccan government and we are working closely together on the problem."

Smugglers! I thought, it sounded like pirate days! *We'll have to keep our eyes open!*

Slowly the view from the limousine changed, the farmland giving way to small houses, packed closely together. The car turned off the highway and suddenly they were in the city of Rabat, moving slowly through the crowded streets. *Now this is a little bit more interesting,* I thought, as I perked up in my seat.

"The Romans founded a town in this area 2000 years ago and Rabat itself has been a thriving city since the 12th century! Some of the roads we are driving on are more than 400 years old!" Aili read excitedly from her new best friend, the guide-book to Morocco.

"Look, over there! At that beautiful wall with the huge door!" Mom said pointing toward the honey colored wall. "That is the ancient wall surrounding the old town, or *medina* as they call it here. I can't wait to do some sightseeing and shopping there!" *Shopping!* I was getting more excited by the minute.

Aili continued reading from her boring book. I really did want to learn about our new country, but it was also fun bugging Aili without getting in trouble for it.

"*Medina*, in Arabic, means a city." Aili looked up, "So San Francisco is a *medina*. But in Moroccan Arabic, the word *medina* usually means the really old part of the town."

"Got it," I said, yawning.

A few minutes later, the limousine glided along a thick stone wall with a large iron gate. Two policemen were posted at the gate, one at each side. The walls were so high it was impossible to see anything except the tops of palm trees growing on the other side.

"Wow!" I said, "Who lives there? The King?"

"Why no, Julia, that is where *you* live!" answered Wayne. "That's Villa America, the Residence of the U.S. Ambassador." And, as if on cue, we turned into the beautiful gravel driveway.

"Are you serious? HAIT!!" Aili said, using *my* expression.

I smiled smugly and fought the urge to say *I told you you'd love it!*

The gates of the residence swung open, and the limousine entered the great courtyard. I gasped. I had thought moving to a place where almost no one spoke English, where we had never been before, that was thousands of miles from our home, would be an adventure. But now, I knew that it would be *much* better than that!

The policemen saluted us as we passed. It was really weird to be so official. I still wasn't totally convinced that this was real and that Ashton Kutcher wasn't about to jump out from a corner and scream, "You've been punk'd!"

The car drove up the gravel driveway, to the front entrance of the residence. The driver jumped out of the limousine and opened the door for us. Mom was the first one out, (she's *always* first, for everything. Moms are like that) followed by Dad, Aili and finally me (why am I always last?). Well technically, Mr. Plant was the last one out, but still.

In the air-conditioned comfort of the limousine, I had not realized that the outside temperature hovered around 85 degrees, and it was sticky. I liked the warmth, but this was ridiculous! I was fanning myself with Aili's guidebook, when I suddenly felt a wonderful cool breeze on my shoulders. I stopped fanning myself flipped open the book to the section entitled "Weather":

> *Rabat, being close to the ocean, is cooled by sea breezes, so although it feels very hot in the sun, in the shade it still feels cool. People call Morocco "a cold country with a hot sun".*

Before I had a chance to read this bit of information out loud, we were walking up the six white marble steps leading up to the entry of Villa America.

Fast as lightning, I opened my tote and grabbed the booklet Mom had given me about Villa America. I only had the chance to read that it was three stories high, and was built in the 1930's before I had to look up. Through the two windows at the front of the house, I caught my first glimpse of our new home. A huge chandelier hung from the high ceiling in the entry hall, its crystals sending sparkling reflections dancing around the room. As we reached the top of the steps, I could see that the wide front door was already open and inside the foyer all the servants were lined up, ready to meet the new Ambassador (my dad) and his family (us!).

Wayne first introduced Mom and Dad, and then made a special point to present us girls to the staff. "Julia and Aili, this is Rashid, the waiter, Kamel, the butler, Zohra and Khadija, the maids and Abdu the cook!"

Aili and I were pretty overwhelmed by all the new faces and strange sounding Moroccan names, but I smiled and began shaking hands (from the right, once again!). Kamel, Rashid and Abdu were wearing white jackets and black pants. The maids, however, were dressed in the Moroccan fashion, wearing long dresses called *caftans* and soft white scarves, or *hijabs*, covering their hair.

"Welcome to Villa America, *Lalla* Julia and *Lalla* Aili" said Kamel warmly. When I looked a little confused by what Kamel had called us, Aili felt obliged to help out, as she had read about this in the guidebook.

"*Lalla* in Arabic is a polite way of addressing girls and women. For example, Mom is '*Lalla* Nancy'", Aili said knowingly, "It is also a title used for Princesses." *Hmmm. Lalla Julia. Princess Julia. It did have a nice ring to it,* I thought.

"It will be so nice to have young people here again," Rashid said. Kamel, Abdu and Rashid spoke very good English, even if they did have pretty strong Moroccan accents. I noticed that after they shook hands with our family, the men then touched their hearts with their right hand. Daddy later said that this was a special way people in Morocco showed respect.

"Thank you, Rashid," said Aili, "*Salaam wa alaykum.*"

Dad had said that everyone in Morocco always greeted each other with *Salaam wa alaykum* (Peace be with you), and Aili and I had rehearsed the greeting many, many times. Now a big smile spread across Aili's face because she had beaten me to the punch (see—last, AGAIN!)

"Excellent! You speak Arabic, *Lalla* Aili!" said Kamel, "*Marhabam beecoom! Labess? Bekhair?*" Aili looked at Kamel and then at me with her mouth open. I tried to stifle a laugh.

"Sorry, Kamel, we are just learning, and we really don't understand Arabic at all! In fact, all we know how to say is what I just said!"

"I can also say *shokran* and *manzaki*n," I announced triumphantly. Aili turned to me, glaring.

"Wonderful, Julia!" Kamel was smiling widely, "You have said *thank you* in Arabic and hello in the Berber language. You have an excellent ear and pronunciation!"

Aili looked at me with darts in her eyes and muttered, "What a show off! It didn't even seem like your were listening to me in the car."

"Things aren't always as they seem," I replied with a smile.

Then we shook hands with Zohra and Khadija, the two maids. Neither Khadija nor Zohra spoke English, although

Zohra spoke a little French. But through warm smiles and the nodding of heads we showed that we were happy to meet each other.

After the introductions, we sat down in our living room for the first time. It wasn't like normal moving, where you move into the house with no furniture. Nope, Villa America was fully furnished. The room was large and airy, with windows on two sides. A fireplace with a marble mantle stood against one wall, and comfortable chairs and sofas were arranged in groups to make conversation easy. The walls were painted a pale yellow, and the upholstered furniture was white. Although most of the furnishings in the room were American (it was an American house after all), there were touches here and there that reminded me we were in Morocco. Against one wall, next to the fireplace, was an antique Moroccan door, hung as though it were a painting. Wayne noticed Mom looking,

"That is a 300 year old door from Marrakech, a city about 4 hours south of here." Wayne explained. Look how thick the wood is! Huge nails are pounded into the door in a precise pattern, and the nail heads make a beautiful decoration, don't they?"

A few minutes later, Rashid appeared from the kitchen carrying a silver tray. On it were five glasses of milk and a bowl full of dates.

"In Morocco, we always greet guests with dates and milk," Rashid smiled as he served the snack.

"How lovely," Mom said she took a date and sipped the milk.

Normally I love milk. But the night before we left for Morocco I had managed to grab Aili's attention with one very interesting fact from the guidebook: some Moroccans drink camel's milk. I tried goat's milk once, and almost had some sort of puke-attack, so I wasn't planning on downing *camel's* milk anytime in my near future.

"Oh," I said, trying to sound casual, "is this camel's milk, Rashid?"

Rashid laughed, "No, *Lalla* Julia! It is cow's milk, but I can get you some camel's milk if you'd like! It is delicious, especially when it is warm, straight from the camel."

"Oh! No, no. Thank you anyway, this is just fine, right Aili?"

"Oh, yes, this is great," she said eagerly. And then she added, "Julia, you can have the camel's milk with dinner!" I giggled nervously and kicked her in the shin.

When we had all finished the milk and dates (the dates were black, sweet and sticky, and looked a little like wrinkled up toes), Dad said, "Well girls, how about exploring the house?"

I was already itching to take a look at my new home, and my guess was that Aili felt the same way. Plus, I wanted to make sure I got first dibs on my choice of bedroom.

"Great!" we said in unison. I put down my milk glass and ran to the big staircase.

"There are four bedrooms and the master bedroom upstairs and a VIP suite down here," Dad called to us, "Choose any room you want upstairs!"

"But not the master bedroom!" Mom added as we raced up the stairs.

At the top of the stairs there was a large landing. Aili and I separated, Aili going one way and I the other.

Each bedroom in the house had a little brass name plaque on it. The bedroom called "Grand Vizier" was painted a pale cream and had two twin beds in it. There were two sets of windows, one overlooking the front of the house, and the other overlooking the back. The "Grand Vizier" shared a bathroom with "La Favorite", a room that looked like it belonged in a French country house. It had a pretty blue and white quilt, antique linens on the night table, lots of pillows and old oil paintings on the wall.

"Oooh! I think I'm going to choose this one!" I mused as I walked around the room looking into the closets and opening the dresser drawers. As I continued to explore the rest of the house, I noticed a small staircase, and raced up it. The room at the top, "Le Poète", was decorated in a Moroccan style with filmy yellow curtains that fluttered in the breeze, and a bold gold, red, purple and blue striped bedspread. Pillows in a riot of colors covered the bed and the two small armchairs. A mosquito net hung over the bed so that it really looked like a bedroom out of Arabian Nights. I knew this was the bedroom I wanted. Make that *had* to have.

"I call Princess *Lalla*!" came a voice from downstairs. I had stopped at that bedroom as well. It was painted a soft mint green and had a ceiling fan and a beautiful Moroccan lantern hanging over the antique French desk. A small tiled balcony overlooked the pool and the garden below. The sun streamed in the window and sparkled off the mirror. The queen size bed was made up with a white coverlet and a pale green flowered comforter. Four big pillows were arranged on the bed, and I could just imagine Aili curled up on them with a good book.

"Hey! Julia, where are you?" I could hear Aili's voice.

"Up here!" I yelled.

"Where?" Aili bellowed again.

"Up here in the tower!" I shouted.

I could see Aili step out onto the balcony of the Princess *Lalla* room, and I waved from the window of the tower.

"Where?" Aili called out yet again, sounding frustrated.

"Up here!" I waved at Aili from the third floor of the house. "This is my room! Come see!"

Aili realized she hadn't even been up to the third floor yet. It could be reached only by the small staircase in the back part of the house. Soon she burst through the door of my room.

"Wow!" Aili breathed.

"Yeah, first come, first served!" I answered. "HAIT! And I've got my own bathroom too!"

I thought about the Princess *Lalla* room with its calm colors and elegant furniture. *Funny how it all works out. Aili is like that room, all quiet and calm.* I felt more like this room—exciting, energetic and spontaneous.

"Let's go check out the garden," I said and together we ran back down the staircase, and down to the ground floor.

Rashid, the waiter, was 28 years old and had worked at Villa America for three years. He had dark hair, was very slender and had a timid yet happy smile. When we got down to the kitchen, he was busy preparing something special in a little silver teapot.

"Hello!" we said together.

"What are you making, Rashid?" I asked.

"Ah, hello *Lalla* Aili and *Lalla* Julia. This is Moroccan mint tea. Everywhere you go in Morocco, you will be offered this special tea in this special pot." I inspected the pot. It was like a regular tea pot, only about 1/3 of the size, and looked like it had been squashed down a bit.

Rashid continued, "You will be offered mint tea in restaurants, at people's homes, even in shops. If you are buying something and you are trying to decide whether or not to get it, the shopkeeper will offer you some mint tea while you think about the purchase."

As he spoke, Rashid took a handful of fresh mint leaves and rinsed them under cold water.

"To make Moroccan tea, we first put green tea and a little bit of boiling water into a small metal teapot. Then we swish it around a bit and pour out the water. This gets rid of the bitter taste of the tea. Then we fill the teapot with water and put it on the stove to boil again. Once it has come to a boil, we take it off the heat and add the mint, like this."

Rashid tore up the mint leaves and placed them in the pot.

"And then we add the sugar. A lot of sugar! Moroccans like sweet things!"

"I love mint!" I said, "May I have a taste?"

"Of course," said Rashid, "But we aren't finished making the tea yet. The final step is to pour out some tea into a glass and then pour that back into the teapot." Rashid poured the tea into a little glass painted with blue and gold designs, and then poured the liquid back into the pot. He did this three times. "Now it is ready!"

The tea was hot, sweet, minty and absolutely delicious. "Yum!" I said, and Aili nodded.

It was fun drinking tea from the little tea glasses instead of the regular teacups we were used to. Taking my glass with me, I walked outside, Aili close behind me. Finally, I was leading the way! Right next to the kitchen was an herb garden with, not surprisingly, huge amounts of mint growing almost wild. The main garden consisted of a lawn area that sloped down to the pool. Lush palm trees, banana plants and bright flowers were carefully tended by two fulltime gardeners. The shimmering swimming pool looked inviting and I sat down on the edge and dangled my feet into the cool blue water.

We waved to our parents who were watching us from the terrace off the master bedroom.

I knew Mom and Dad were worried about us, about our liking Morocco. But at that moment, drinking mint tea, sitting by the pool, in the warm sun, I knew the magic of Morocco was already casting its spell on us.

Aili got up and started to walk toward the back of the garden. I was about to join her when I noticed a man bending over to pick up and carry our luggage into the house. "*Shokran,*" I said and smiled warmly to him. The man straightened up and stared back at me. The jagged scar on his left cheek, those scary eyes … it was the weird man from the airport! I gasped, and turned around to catch up with Aili.

"Look!" I whispered and pointed toward the house. "It's him, Scarface!"

Aili looked over to where I was pointing. By now the man was walking into the house with the luggage.

"Weird," she muttered. "I wonder what he does …"

"And why do we seem to see him everywhere?"

5

Aili

The first day of school is always hard but it's even harder when it's in the middle of a school year, in a brand new school and in a brand new *country*. The night before, I had worried about what to wear to school, wondering if my Palo Alto clothes would be OK. Would the same stuff that was considered cute in America be cool here? But when we got to school and looked around, I saw that there was no need to be concerned. The students wore everything, from American styles to trendy European fashions to traditional Muslim clothes. Some of the girls covered their hair with scarves, *hijabs*, but most of them did not.

The teachers at the Rabat American School (or "RAS" as people called it) were all really helpful and welcoming. Although it was called the Rabat *American* School, most of the students were Moroccans, French, English, and six other nationalities. Actually, there were only a handful of Americans, and most of them had parents who worked at the Embassy. The school had all 12 grades, and Julia was the newest 6ᵗʰ grader and I was the newest 8ᵗʰ grader.

I was super relieved when I realized that the classwork wasn't that much different from the classwork at home. Except, of course, for Arabic class. Everyone had to learn Arabic and one other language. For many of the students, the second language was English. But Mom had naturally insisted that Julia and I not go the easy route by taking the English classes. Instead, we had to choose another language. Both of us chose French.

"What a great choice," Mom said, "Did you know that French is the third language of Morocco? Morocco was under French rule for about 40 years. That is why so many people here speak Arabic, Berber and French. Imagine! They speak three languages, while so many Americans only speak one. But that's changing now in the U.S. which is wonderful!"

We knew that line by heart. Our mother, who spoke five languages, always told us how important it was to speak many languages: "It makes you a citizen of the world, not just of the United States," she would tell us.

At lunchtime that first day of school, Julia and I headed to the cafeteria, our stomachs rumbling with hunger. When we got in line, however, we were surprised that there was not a PB and J, or tuna sandwich in sight. No burgers or tacos, either. Instead there was a white, fluffy looking thing topped with vegetables.

"Here you go," said the server standing behind the counter as she loaded our trays with the food, "*Bon appétit.*"

We looked at each other glumly.

"What *is* this?" I asked Julia as I stared at what looked like chopped up rice.

"I don't know, but I'd rather have a burger," Julia murmured softly, "I don't even know how you are supposed to eat this stuff." We knew better than to complain out loud (Mom would be so mad!) but there was no way we were going to eat this.

"Why can't they just have regular food?" Julia asked.

We walked over to a table and sat down staring at the stuff on our trays.

"Just try it! You may even like it!" came a voice from behind us.

I jumped, and turned around to see a tall girl with long dark brown hair tied with a pretty blue ribbon. She smiled at us and her green eyes sparkled.

"Hi! My name is Abla. I'm in 8th grade."

"Hi, I'm Aili, and this is Julia. She's in 6th and I'm in 8th too!" I was relieved to meet someone my age so soon.

Abla slid her tray onto the table next to mine and said, "You were probably hoping for a McDonald's or something," Abla smiled as she spoke, "Well, we do have a MacDoe (as they call it here) in Rabat, but not at this cafeteria. That on your plate is called *Couscous*. It's practically the national food of Morocco. Everyone eats it, especially on Fridays, even though sometimes we have it on other days too, like today. It's made out of wheat and tastes sort of like very fluffy rice. Today they topped it with a vegetable stew, but sometimes they top it with chicken, lamb, and other things. It really is good. Try it!" Abla started eating.

"How do you know so much about it, Abla?"

"Well, I was born in Morocco, and lived in Algeria for a few years. Couscous is eaten all over North Africa."

Gingerly, I loaded my fork with a little couscous and some of the vegetables. As I brought the fork to my mouth, Julia studied me carefully.

"Go ahead, Aili! I'm just going to watch!"

I placed the food in my mouth and started to chew. Suddenly, I opened my eyes wide, clutched my throat and started to moan, "Ohhhhh!! Ohhhhhh!"

"Oh my Gosh! Help her! Help her!" Julia cried, "Aili, Aili are you ok?" Julia was beginning to panic.

I turned to her, my eyes still wide, and slowly dropped my hands from my throat, trying to hold a straight face.

"Of course I am, Julia! The couscous is delicious!"

I burst out laughing, and Abla joined in. Julia was mortified at being made to look foolish, and decided she really didn't like this Abla girl very much.

"You should have seen the look on your face, Julie!" said Abla, "It was priceless! Go ahead, your turn to try the couscous."

"My name is Juli*a*, and I don't think that was a funny joke. And I don't like the couscous."

"You haven't even tried it … it's fun to try new things!" Abla protested.

"I know I don't like it … and I don't have to try it." Julia threw her fork on the tray, and pushed it away.

"Fine," I said, somewhat surprised by Julia's stubborn and rude behavior. "You can just go hungry. You don't know what you are missing!" Abla started giggling again.

"There really is such a difference between 11 and 13," I said to Abla. Julia was trying to ignore us, but I could tell she was getting angrier and angrier by the minute.

"Great. Aili has a new best friend and I'm all alone," Julia tried to say under her breath.

"I *heard* you, Julia!" I nudged her

Abla and I had a great time talking throughout lunch, but Julia stayed mostly quiet. I knew she felt left out.

Abla explained to me how her stepfather was a really important Algerian businessman who was setting up a new business in Morocco. She said that her mother was the most beautiful woman in the world, but was living in the countryside, outside of Fez, one of the oldest cities in Morocco. I could tell that Julia thought Abla was really bragging, but she listened, fascinated, as Abla told us all about her life.

"Our house here in Rabat was once a palace," Abla said. Julia rolled her eyes. Julia was obviously not happy with the way Abla and I were hitting it off.

"Wow! That's so cool, Abla! You have the best life!" I said.

"Well ... I guess so ... but I really wish I could be with my mother."

"Why aren't you?"

"My father died when I was very little, and my mother married Aziz, my stepfather about two years ago. She was not really happy living in a city, so she moved to the countryside about a month ago. There are no good schools there so my mother said it would be better for me to finish the school year here at RAS and then move with her to the country. So right now I am living with Aziz. He's OK, I guess, but I just miss my mother."

Abla was quiet for a minute. I wasn't sure what to say. I felt sorry for my new friend, but wondered why Abla couldn't just visit her mother. They sounded very rich.

Then suddenly Abla perked up. "Hey! Why don't you come over Friday after school for a visit? You can meet my pet ... we'll go for a swim! Aziz will probably not be there ... he travels so much."

"Who takes care of you, then, when he's gone?" I asked.

"I have a *Dada* who has looked after me since I was born ... like a second mother, really."

"Your *Dada* is your second *mother*?" Julia laughed.

"Yes, Julia. *Dada* is the word in Arabic for a nanny," Abla explained, "So what do you say? Please come over! It would be so fun!"

"Well, I have to make sure it is ok with my parents, but I would love to come over!" I exclaimed excitedly.

Julia muttered something under he breath and frowned.

"So, it's a plan! See you Friday after school, Aili!"

I could tell Julia felt totally abandoned. "Great," Julia whispered to me, "Abla seems like such a mean girl. I really don't like her."

Abla got up from the table and picked up her tray.

"And Julia, I am going to make you some special Moroccan food on Friday when you come over. You'll love my pet too. His name is Maco and he's a monkey! See you both later!"

"OK Abla!" Julia exclaimed, a broad smile on her face. "I knew I liked her, Aili. But she really is a liar ... no way she lives in a palace and double no way she has a real monkey!"

I got up from the table and said, "Well, I had better head to my next class. Are you coming Julia?"

"You go ahead, I need to get my books organized," Julia answered.

I walked out of the cafeteria, but watched Julia through the window in the door. I was too smart to know she wasn't about to *organize her books* ... I watched her take a little bite of her abandoned couscous. She slowly swallowed, nodded and continued to eat bigger spoonfuls with each bite. I smiled and walked briskly to my next class, not wanting to be late.

6

Julia

The next morning at breakfast, Aili and I chatted excitedly about the previous day at school and all we had learned.

"Hey Mom! Guess which country was the first to recognize the U.S. after the American Revolution in 1776? I know Daddy knows ..." I challenged.

"Well, let's see, was it France?" Mom guessed. "They helped the Americans in our Revolutionary war against England, so I guess they would have been the first ones to recognize that we were a new country."

"Nope! It was Morocco!" interrupted Aili.

"Aili! I was the one asking the question.... why do you always wreck it for me?" I complained.

"I didn't wreck anything. I just knew the answer. What is the big de ...?"

"Please girls! Stop! I think it is wonderful that you are both learning about our host country," interjected Dad diplomatically. "Isn't it interesting how Morocco has been a friend to the United States for over 200 years? When you think that when the U.S. was just a new nation, Morocco had already thousands of years of history, it's pretty amazing. Imagine, the *medina* was already an ancient place when America and England fought in the Revolutionary War!"

"In fact," added Mom, "when Europe entered the Dark Ages, the people of North Africa, who today are the Moroccans, Algerians, Tunisians and Libyans, were the ones that preserved a lot of knowledge. While the Europeans were burning books, the North Africans were preserving them."

Mom then turned to me and asked, "Julia, what is your favorite subject?"

"Math! You know that, mom!" I answered.

"Well, did you know that Algebra was developed by the Arabs?"

"Another thing to be thankful for," Aili murmured. Aili excelled in History and English, but struggled in Math. While Aili, Mom and Dad continued talking about Moroccan history, I tuned out for a minute and gazed out the window, into the beautiful garden. The stone fountain, present in so many Moroccan homes, gurgled peacefully, as birds flitted about, drinking and cooling themselves in the sparkling water.

It really is beautiful here, I thought to myself. An incurable romantic, I liked reading books about princesses, pirates and castles. *I can just imagine a princess living here and looking out at the garden from this same window.*

I awoke from my daydream when I spotted two men standing about 30 feet away, at the base of the large stone wall that surrounded the garden. They were talking to each other and suddenly looked up when they sensed me watching them. Without saying another word, they walked away in opposite directions. One of the men turned back and glanced in my direction. As he turned to look at me, I recognized him immediately. Again, Scarface! *What was going on here?* We kept seeing this man over and over, in the VIP lounge, at the airport curbside, with our luggage. Our eyes met, and then he turned and quickly walked away.

Creepy, I thought. I was about to ask Dad about him when I tuned back into the conversation and realized that Mom, Dad and Aili were talking about Abla. I jumped right in.

"Hey, you know what? Abla says they live in a palace and have a huge pool and travel all over the place *AND*, sorry, but I don't believe it …" I paused for effect, "*AND* she says they have a monkey for a pet!" I rolled my eyes.

"Julia!" Aili retorted, "Why would she lie about that? She invited us over, and if we can go, we'll see for ourselves! Mom, Dad, would it be ok if we go to her house? She invited us to come on Friday to stay and have dinner with her."

"I think that will be fine," said Dad looking at Mom, "but we just need to have the Embassy security people here check it out first. Do you have her last name and the address?"

"She gave me this card. It's her stepdad's business card. Is that enough?" Aili asked. I hoped that it was, because deep down I really wanted to go.

"Sure. Let me give it to the Regional Security Officer, the RSO, at the Embassy and he will check it out."

On Friday morning, Aili and I got up extra early so we could accompany our cook, Abdu, on his excursion to the outdoor market in the *medina*, or old town of Rabat. At first I was over-whelmed by the exotic (and pretty stinky) smells coming from the *medina*. It was a mixture of spices, straw, and ...

"What *is* that funky smell, Julia?" Aili asked.

At that moment the answer crossed right in front of us: a donkey carrying baskets filled with tangerines made its way down the narrow street. Let's just say it was *not* the tangerines that were the cause of the foul smells ...

"Oh, yeah, that's it," I said, scrunching up my nose and pointing at the donkey, "the smell is spices mixed with donkeys ... and donkey ... stuff ..."

Although it was not the best of smells, we soon got used to it and enjoyed discovering the *medina* with Abdu. The crooked medieval streets of the old town were lined with hundreds of *hanoots* (stalls) crammed with exotic spices, olives, nuts, fruits and vegetables. As we passed the shops, the owners would cry out, "*Labess! Bekhair!* Welcome welcome! I have the best olives in Rabat!" or "Come in my *hanoot* for the finest spices from the four corners of the world!"

Everyone seemed to know Abdu as he made his way through the *medina*, stopping here and there, gathering the ingredients he would turn into tonight's fabulous meal.

"Labess *Haj* Abdu! *Haj! Bekhair! Salaam wa alaykum, Haj* Abdu!" they called out to him. Smiling broadly, Abdu waved to them and touched his hand to his heart.

"I thought your name was Abdu! But they're all calling you *Haj*!" I said as we made out way through the medina.

Abdu laughed, "*Haj* is just a title I have, a great honor. It is because I went on a pilgrimage to Mecca, the city in Saudi Arabia where out prophet Mohammed was born. At least once in a Muslim's life, he should try to make this trip, also called a *Haj*.

It is one of the five pillars, the five basic beliefs of our religion, *Islam.*"

I noticed some of the streets in the *medina* were so narrow, no cars could possibly squeeze through. So, just as it had been for the last 500 years, the food and other products sold in the *medina* arrived via carts pulled either by men or by donkeys. Women, with huge baskets filled with fruits, plodded their way through the maze of streets. Men balanced huge trays of freshly baked bread on their heads, making their way from the bakeries to the cafes and restaurants of the *medina.* Aili and I were fascinated by what we saw, until we came to the lady seated on the ground, with a cage full of pigeons.

"How neat!" I cried, "She's selling pet pigeons! I would love to get one! It is so unfair that we don't have any pets, and I really miss Bailey. Please, Abdu, can we get a pet pigeon?"

Abdu only shook his head and laughed. "*Lalla* Julia," he explained, "these are not for pets! These pigeons are for eating! *Jooj, afek.* I will take two," he said to the pigeon lady, "I put these pigeons into a traditional Moroccan dish called *pastilla*, a flaky crusted pigeon pie, flavored with almonds and raisins. You will try it tonight!"

I looked at Aili, horrified. The thought of eating pigeon made me sick, *especially* one that I could see alive right now.

"Oh, it's too bad, Abdu," I remembered quickly, "we are going to our friend Abla's house tonight!"

"Well then I shall save you both a piece and you may have it in the morning. *Pastilla* for breakfast will be an extra special treat!"

I made a mental note to tell Mom and Dad to be sure to eat *all* the pigeon pie at dinner tonight.

We continued walking through the *medina*, and I noticed that Abdu would stop now and then and hand out a few coins to beggars on the street.

"This is another of the five pillars of our religion, *Islam*," Abdu explained, "In Islam, we believe that it is important to give money to those who are less fortunate than ourselves. That is called giving alms to the poor."

"What are the other pillars, Abdu?" I asked, curious about the religion of Morocco.

"Well, as you have probably already seen, we must pray to *Allah*, God, five times a day."

I remembered that when we first got to Morocco, I would be awakened every morning around 4 AM by the voices calling the Muslims to the first morning prayer. It was pretty loud, because the call to prayer came from all the mosques and was broadcast on loudspeakers. I was used to it now, and it didn't always wake me up. I also knew Muslims prayed at noon, in the afternoon, at sunset and at night.

I counted to myself: 1) Pray five times a day, 2) Give alms, 3) Make the *Haj*. "So what are the other two pillars?" I asked.

"We must profess the faith, which means we must say each day that there is only one God, *Allah*, and that Mohammed is his prophet."

"And the fifth?"

"Ah, the fifth pillar of Islam is that we must observe Ramadan. But I will tell you about that later. Right now I must get back to Villa America so I can start preparing the *pastilla*!"

7

Aili

In most of the Islamic world, the workweek starts on Saturday and goes through Wednesday. Thursday and Friday, the Holy Day, are the weekend days when stores and offices are closed. But this isn't the case in Morocco. Because the French ruled Morocco for many years, Morocco follows the European system of a Monday through Friday workweek. So, the last day of the week for school was Friday, just like at home in the U.S.

On this particularly beautiful Friday afternoon Julia and I were excited because we would be spending it with our new friend, Abla. We had agreed to meet at the front of the school as soon as classes were over. Julia and Abla were already waiting when I showed up at the front gate. I could only hope Julia wasn't telling Abla any embarrassing secrets about me!

After a few minutes, a Mercedes limousine pulled up. A uniformed chauffeur jumped out, tipped his hat to Abla and then to Julia and me, and opened the car door. Julia glanced at me as Abla said, "*Shokran, Si* Mohamed," and got into the car. "Come on, guys!" she called to us, "I can hardly wait to go for a swim!" Julia and I jumped in, and the car sped off.

"I noticed you said to the driver *Si* Mohamed, Abla," I said as we drove through the leafy streets of Rabat, "What does *Si* mean?"

"Oh, well, you know how girls and women are called *Lalla*? Well, *Si* is short for *Sidi*, which is a term of respect for a man. Like your father is '*Sidi* Thomas'." Abla continued her explanation, "Normally, since he is our servant, I would just call the driver by his first name, without the *Si*. But because his name is 'Mohamed', the name of the Prophet, the founder of our religion of Islam, we always say '*Si*', out of respect."

"So, even if you see a little boy, or a baby, and his name is Mohamed, you would call him '*Si*' Mohamed?" Julia asked.

"That's right, Julia! I can SEE you figured it out right away!" We all groaned at Abla's pun.

"Wow!" Julia whispered to me as the car approached a massive marble building, "Abla's house is even bigger than our house!"

The three-story, red-tiled house was enormous, surrounded by lush gardens filled with hibiscus, geraniums and brightly colored bougainvillea. Ornamental ponds and fountains cooled them, and the intricate Moroccan tile work, or *zeleej*, brightened the walls and gates. The car pulled up to the front steps, and Abla popped out before the chauffeur had a chance to open the door for her.

"Come on!" Abla motioned toward the mansion. She bounded up the steps, through the massive door and waited for us to follow her. "Fatima, we're here!" Abla shouted, "We're going to change and then go for a swim!"

"Wow! Your house is gorgeous!" I said as I followed Abla toward the enormous marble staircase that led to the bedrooms. The staircase, covered by oriental carpets, curved gracefully upward toward a central landing. Two hallways led from the landing to the eight bedrooms and bathrooms.

"Yeah," Julia agreed, making her way up the stairs. She then whispered to me, "I guess I really was wrong about the *palace* part of Abla's story …"

Just as she was talking to me, I could see two furry little hands grab at Julia's shoulders from behind. Julia felt it just as I saw it and we both jumped back, frightened.

"What? Hey! What … Hey!" Julia screamed. Her hands instinctively went to her shoulders and reached for the stranger's hands. What she felt caused her to scream again. The creature with the tiny, brown and furry hands was now sitting on her shoulders!

"Maco! Maco!" Abla laughed, "What are you doing, you silly monkey! Get off of Julia!"

The monkey jumped off of Julia and onto the banister where he showed off by swinging by one arm.

"Oh my gosh! Abla! You *do* have a monkey! Oh my gosh, this is the cutest pet in the *whole* world!" Then probably thinking of our dog Bailey, Julia quickly added, "Well, *one* of the cutest. How fun! How long have you had him Abla?"

At this point, Maco was bored with swinging and jumped into his mistress' arms. Abla held him like a baby.

"I've had him for about a year," she said as she scratched his little head, "Aziz, my stepfather, found him on one of his trips. He had been part of a village circus, and the people who were supposed to care for him were really mean. He was skinny, had lots of missing fur, and for a while we thought he wasn't going to make it. But we nursed him back to health, and now he's more fun than ... well ... more fun than a barrel of monkeys!"

"Now I really know what I want for a pet," Julia said, "Aili isn't he the greatest?" Julia stepped toward Abla and beckoned for Maco to come to her. Without any hesitation he did so, and Julia looked like she was in heaven.

The four of us (Julia, Abla, Maco and I) climbed the huge staircase as we made our way to Abla's room. Like the rest of the house, the bedroom was enormous—two French doors led to a terrace overlooking the garden. The walls were covered with pale blue and white striped wallpaper, and blue and white flow-ered draperies framed the windows. A queen-sized bed was against the wall to the right, covered with the same material as the draperies. On the highly polished wood floor lay two blue area rugs, and the white furniture completed the picture of the perfect room.

"Oh, Abla, this is wonderful. I would never want to leave if this were *my* room! You are so lucky," I said as I sat down on the fluffy duvet covering her bed.

"Yeah, *real* lucky," answered Abla, "my mother is off living in the countryside, and my stepfather is always traveling or doing his business. Sometimes I think the only one who really cares about me in this world is Maco ..."

She turned to me with a glum face and looked as if she were about to cry, but then just as quickly she laughed and shrieked, "Time for the pool!"

Julia and I took off our backpacks and pulled out our swimsuits. Julia quickly changed into her pink two-piece, and followed Abla to the pool. I wanted a turn to play with Maco, so I said I would join them in a few minutes.

"Come on, Maco!" I said as soon as the girls left the room, "Do you want to play?"

I reached for his hand, but the monkey wriggled away from my grasp and ambled to the bedroom door. He paused for a moment, looked at me and scampered down the hall. At the top of the stairs, he paused again, as if waiting for me.

"Oh! So you want to play 'follow the leader'! Ok, let's go!"

I followed Maco down the stairs, and into the impressive foyer toward the entry to the pool area. Through the windows, I could see Julia and Abla already splashing about in the pool.

"Ok, Maco. Let's go to the pool!" I said. But Maco had other ideas. He scurried toward another door, a small wooden one that was half-hidden under the staircase.

"Maco! Come back here!" I was now getting tired of the little game, and wanted to go for a swim.

But Maco refused to come. Instead, he pushed on the small door, which opened just slightly. From inside the room, I could hear a man's voice.

"I don't know what you are talking about, Aziz. I have always been fiercely loyal. You must believe …" the voice trailed off.

Curiosity getting the better of me, I walked to where Maco was standing and peered into the room. I gasped. Almost every inch of wall space was covered with animal heads or hides. There were tiger and leopard skins; large antlers and elephant tusks; a stuffed cheetah stood in the corner, on top of a rug that looked like it may have once been a lion.

These all look like endangered animals! I thought to myself, remembering what I had learned at the San Francisco Zoo and in a special unit in my Social Studies class.

Alligator heads grinned hideously from their mounts on the walls. On a small table with a glass top dozens of ivory carvings were displayed. Then I noticed the legs of the coffee table ... they were made from elephant hoofs. I just couldn't believe what I was seeing. The whole room looked like it was filled with endangered animal hides and parts, or at least with animals that should be freely roaming the grasslands of Africa rather than decorating a rich man's office. I shuddered and looked down. As I lifted my head, I noticed a man's profile reflected in a mirror. He was standing at the opposite end of the room, and was talking to someone who was just out of my sight. I held my breath as I got a clear view of him. The dark bird-like eyes, the angry scar on his face ... it was the man from the embassy!

"I don't want excuses!" the man who was out of sight was speaking softly, but was clearly upset. "You do what I tell you to do!"

"Don't worry, we will soon be adding to your collection."

"It is not *my* collection I'm worried about. If that shipment doesn't go out, my buyers in China will find another seller. There is too much money in it for me to lose out on this. All we need is the signed paperwork."

My mind was racing. Why was the man with the scar at this house? Something was very wrong, something shady was going on, and I was frightened. Holding Maco in my arms, I backed away from the door as quietly as I could, and then ran to the pool where Abla and Julia were playing "Marco Polo." I rushed toward Julia and said, "We have to go *now*".

"What? Why? You haven't even swum yet!" Julia exclaimed.

"We just have to go, Julia! Come on!"

"Why do we have to go? I want to stay!" she pleaded.

"Julia! We have to! Come on! I'll call home and see if Mom can send a driver to pick us up."

I stood on the edge of the pool, my face pale. I was breathing heavily and Julia could see that something was wrong. So could Abla.

"Ok, ok. Abla, I'm so sorry," Julia said as she got out of the pool. Then she turned to me and whispered, "You'd better have a good reason for this, Aili."

Julia went into the house to change, and I tried to explain my sudden departure to Abla. "I'm sorry," I said awkwardly, "We … just have to go. I … I'm sorry."

"But why do you want to leave, Aili?" Abla asked sadly. She sounded so disappointed that I almost felt sorry for her. But at the same time I realized that Abla lived in the house, so she had to know what was in that room, and that meant she had to know about killing all those endangered animals. That made me feel disgusted. So it wasn't hard to pretend that I had a head-ache, a *very* bad headache.

"I'm sorry, Abla, I just feel sick. Maybe we could come back another time."

"Oh, I'm sorry you're not feeling good," Abla said, but I was not sure she believed me, "I hope you feel better really soon."

"Thanks, and … sorry," I stammered.

"So you and Julia will come swimming another time," Abla said hopefully, "And don't worry about calling your Mom. Si Mohamed will take you home."

By the time Julia had dressed and we went to the front of the house, Abla's car and driver were already waiting for us.

"Bye Abla. Thank you. See you at school," Julia waved sadly.

But before we could get into the car, Maco came scampering toward Julia and jumped onto her backpack. He was already opening the flap when Abla cried out, "Maco Stop! You silly monkey!" She reached out and pulled him off the backpack. "Sorry, Julia. I always keep bananas for him in my backpack. So now, every time he sees a backpack he thinks there is something in it for him to eat!"

"No problem," Julia grinned as she petted Maco, "He is such a cute monkey. Next time I'll have a treat for him."

We kissed each other goodbye, Moroccan style: first on the right cheek, then twice on the left cheek. But as I kissed Abla I couldn't help think to myself *how could Abla have such a cute pet and not be bothered by all the dead animals in that room?*

The chauffeur opened the car door and we got in. As we drove away, I saw Abla and Maco waving goodbye. I also saw a man, standing at a window watching us, a grim look on his face.

8

Julia

Once safely back at Villa America, Aili explained to me what she had seen. She had not dared to even speak of it in the car, for fear that Abla's driver would overhear her.

"There must be some mistake, Aili," I said, "Abla does not seem like someone whose stepfather would be involved in the hunting and killing of endangered animals to make money from their skins!"

"I know, I know. But I also know what I saw. Julia, it was horrible!" Aili was visibly distressed from what she had seen less than an hour before.

While she was speaking, she turned on her computer. She clicked open Internet Explorer and Googled the words "endangered animals" + "Africa". 223,000 web pages came up, so she refined her search by adding "trade". Up popped just what she was looking for: the World Wildlife Fund page talking about endangered wildlife www.worldwildlife.org.

"There! You see! It says right here that there are still groups of evil people who hunt and kill endangered species and sell their body parts." She read further. "They sell to rich people who can't think of anything better than to wear a coat made out of a poor cheetah skin. How disgusting is that!"

HDIT is right, I thought to myself. "But Aili, Morocco doesn't have any of these kinds of animals," I said looking at pictures of poor elephants and rhinos. "These kinds of animals are in the other parts of Africa, south of the Sahara Desert, a long way from here."

"I know, Julia", Aili sounded exasperated, "but remember what Mr. Plant said, for centuries Morocco has been used by smugglers because of its great ports like Casablanca and because it is so close to Europe. Remember, Tangier is only seventeen miles from Spain, just across the Mediterranean Sea!"

Aili scrolled down the page some more and stopped at a picture of a dead elephant lying in an open field. "Look! Here it says that some hunters kill an entire elephant just to take its tusks to make ivory carvings and other trinkets. They just leave the elephant body to rot in the jungle."

I was reading over Aili's shoulder. "This is really awful! It says here that elephants actually grieve when they find a body of a family member. How can Abla's stepfather be so cruel?" I wondered aloud.

"Well, we can't be sure he's selling endangered animal parts," Aili said, "but I think we should tell Dad what we suspect."

We found Dad in his study, listening to his Arabic tapes.

"*Marhabam! Marhabam beecoom,*" he said, practicing how to say "welcome" in Arabic. Then again, "*Marhabam beecoom.*"

I smiled to myself. After only a few weeks of Arabic at school and practicing with Abdu, our pronunciation was much better than Dad's. But I would never tell him.

"Dad, can we interrupt you for a second?" I asked.

"Sure girls! Hey, I thought you were at Abla's!"

"We were, Dad, and that's what we want to talk to you about," Aili began.

When we finished our story, Dad sat back and was silent for a few seconds.

"Mr. Ahmed is a very important Algerian businessman, who has come to Morocco to set up factories. These factories are very important to Morocco because they will provide a lot of jobs, and help people live better. In fact, I met with him to discuss his plans. He seems like a very reasonable, likeable man. I cannot believe he would be involved in something like this."

"But Dad, what about all the animals on the walls and on the floors?" Aili questioned.

"Maybe those things were in the house already when he bought it and he didn't have time to get rid of them. *Or* maybe they are fakes, copies of animal skins. That's not uncommon, girls."

"Well," I replied, "I know if I had been in the house I would've gotten rid of them the first thing. Real or fake, they're sickening."

"And what about the guy with the scar? I am sure it is that man we saw here at Villa America with the luggage, and also at the airport," Aili asked.

"Aili, that's impossible. It wasn't the same man," Dad answered matter-of-factly.

"But Dad! I saw him!" Aili protested.

"You must have been mistaken," Dad said again. As he spoke, he took some notes. "Listen, girls, I really do thank you so much for telling me about this, but I am sure there is nothing to worry about. Now, I have to keep studying my Arabic. I am expected to make a speech tomorrow night at the Moroccan-American Friendship League and I would like to make some of it in Arabic!"

"But Dad!" I couldn't believe he wasn't bothered by what we had just told him.

"It's fine, girls. I'll talk to you later," and with that he picked up his headphones and continued his Arabic practice.

As we walked out of our father's study, I wanted to believe he was right. "Maybe it's like the figures in Madame Tussaud's wax museum in London, Aili. The animal heads could *look* really real, but could have been made from wax and stuff."

"I guess," Aili said uncertainly, but in my heart I was not convinced.

9

Aili

"Marrakech?" Julia repeated, "We're going to Marrakech?"

"Yes, if you like!" said Mom as she served Dad a second helping of Moroccan pancakes at breakfast one Tuesday morning a few weeks later. "I just got a letter from the school, and they've organized a weekend field trip to Marrakech for interested students."

"Please pass the honey," I said. I loved to slather the pancakes the Moroccan way, with lots and lots of butter and honey. "That is so cool! Marrakech. We've already learned a little about it in Social Studies."

"Madame Bernoussi will be leading the group," Dad added.

"Madame Bernoussi?" Mom looked questioningly at Dad, "I thought she had been ... well ... sort of fired from the Embassy."

"Well, it is true that things didn't work out that well with her. But the school is giving her another chance. She was born in Marrakech and knows the city and its special secrets. She'll be a great leader to the Rose City," Dad said.

Marrakech, an ancient city dating back almost 1000 years, had many names: 'The Rose City' because almost all of the buildings are painted the same deep pink color; 'The Gateway to the Sahara', because of its location near the beginning of the Sahara Desert; and 'Jewel of the South' because of its glittering beauty.

"There's a lot of great history and culture in Marrakech," Mom said, and then looking at us added, "and fabulous shopping in the ancient *medina!*"

"*Hamdullah!*" Julia and I both cried out at the same time.

Hamdullah was one of those great Moroccan expressions that we use all the time. It literally means "Praise God", but people use it all the time to mean "Great" or "Thank Goodness". I also loved to say *makain mooshkil*, which meant "no problem". It was always so much fun to say: "*makain mooshkil, makain mooshkil*".

During lunch at school that day, everyone was talking about the upcoming field trip. Abla, Julia and I sat together and discussed our plans.

"We definitely have to get a room together. The *three* of us," Julia emphasized. We still felt bad about that afternoon at the pool and wanted to make it up to Abla.

"Yeah!" chimed in Abla.

"It'll be so fun! I'm already thinking about what to buy," I said. I pulled out a little notebook and started to write down ideas. One page in the notebook for gifts for friends, one page for gifts for family and one page for me.

"In the *medina* you can get really great silver jewelry for cheap. I got some dangly earrings with little beads on them last time I was there. They were only two dirhams each! That's about twenty U.S. cents!" Abla explained.

"You're kidding! That's so cheap!" I wrote down "earrings" on each of the pages, friends, family, and self.

"Aili is always so organized," Julia said as she peered over my shoulder to see what I was writing.

"They also have these great silky scarves and, of course, millions of *baboosh*," Abla continued.

"*Baboosh*? Those pointy slippers?" Julia asked.

"Yeah, everyone in Morocco wears them. They're really comfortable and the bright yellow leather is great," Abla explained, taking a bite of lemon flavored chicken.

"I hope we can get a good price on the *baboosh* too, like the earrings," I said.

"*Makain mooshkil*," said Abla, "You know, in Morocco we never pay the first price."

"What do you mean you don't pay the first price?" asked Julia, "Don't you just pay whatever the price is?"

"Well, no," Abla began, "In many shops in Morocco there is no fixed price, and prices are not marked. You have to bargain back and forth with the shopkeeper to see how much you will pay. For example, if you want to buy a dress you say, "*How much is this dress?*" The shopkeeper says "*500 dirhams.*" Then you say, "*No, I like the dress, but I can only pay 200 dirhams.*" He says "*Not 200 dirhams. You pay 300 dirhams.*" Then you say, "*Ok, I will pay 250 dirhams. That is my final price.*" Then the shopkeeper says ok, you say ok, and you buy it! That's sort of how it works!"

Shopping in Morocco wasn't going to be like shopping at the Stanford Shopping Center in Palo Alto, that's for sure! I wonder what the saleslady at Nordstrom's would say if I told her I was only willing to give her $15 for a $25 tee-shirt!

"You mean you have to bargain for everything?" Julia asked.

"When you are in the *medina*, the old town, then most of the shops will bargain. But of course, there are larger shops and big malls like you have in America, where there are fixed prices."

"Bargaining sounds like fun!" Julia said, looking like she was ready to go up against the shopkeepers and get the best price she possibly could.

"Remember that in Marrakech," continued Abla, "the first price will be very high. Much worse than here in Rabat. You should end up paying only about *half* of what the shopkeeper tells you first. But remember, the key to bargaining is to keep it friendly, and after you bargain and decide on a price, you have to buy!"

We chatted on excitedly about the trip. What to wear (Marrakech in late May would be hot and dry, maybe as high as 100 degrees) what we would see (ancient monuments dating back 800 years or more) and what we would buy (jewelry and shoes topped the list).

"By the way, Abla," Julia said after a while, "how's Maco? Still jumping on backpacks trying to steal food?"

"Yup. That's Maco. Naughty but nice!"

Finally, the great excursion day arrived! Mom and Dad dropped Julia and me off at the train station (5:15 AM for the 5:45 AM train!) where we waited with the thirty or so other student from RAS for the Marrakech train.

We had packed our bags carefully: one suitcase each (not too full, since we planned on filling it up with goodies we would buy in Marrakech) and a back pack each containing the things we would need for he train ride: a few small snacks, a guide book, pen, pad of paper, gum, money, ID and train pass. And of course, Julia brought her tape recorder! The train ride was going to take about four and a half hours, heading south and passing through beautiful Moroccan countryside.

We chatted with the other kids from school and looked around anxiously for Abla. Finally we saw her, getting out of her limousine with Maco while her chauffeur struggled to get her luggage out of the trunk.

"Hi!" Julia yelled out, "Over here, Abla!"

Abla looked up and waved, and started to head toward us. Julia rushed toward her, hoping to get a chance to play with Maco a little before the train left.

"Maco! Maco!" Julia cried out, "Come here!"

Maco looked toward Julia, and, spotting her backpack ran to her and jumped onto it.

"You are one smart monkey!" Julia laughed, "Yeah, this time I do have something in my backpack!"

Maco opened the flap and reached down with his hand and pulled out a plastic bag filled with raisins. Julia smiled, amazed as the monkey slid open the plastic zip lock. He grabbed a handful of raisins and ate them chewing quickly and watching Julia the whole time.

"That's ok, Maco! The raisins are for you!" Julia poked him gently in the belly.

While Julia played with Maco, I ran over to Abla.

"Are you ready?" I asked excitedly.

"I sure am!" Abla hugged me.

Leaning against Abla's limousine, stood a man who appeared to be watching me very closely. He was clad in a brilliant white *jelleba*, the long robe men wear in North Africa. Usually made of a lightweight cotton, the *jelleba* is perfect for keeping you as cool as possible in the hot sun. He stared at me for a moment, and then a flicker of recognition seemed to cross his face and he turned slightly pale. Just as quickly, however, he seemed to regain his composure and called out, "Abla! Come here, if you please." Abla turned around and returned to the man at the limo.

I couldn't hear the discussion, but from the stricken look on Abla's face as she walked back towards us I knew something was very wrong.

"I can't go," Abla said tearfully when she returned, "Aziz says I can't go! He says I must stay here. I ... I ... can't go to Marrakech ... I ..." She sobbed and didn't finish her sentence, but just turned away and ran toward the waiting limo.

"What was that all about?" Julia, who was still playing with Maco, looked questioningly at me.

"I don't know," I answered, "but I'm guessing that man was Abla's stepdad, Aziz."

I shuddered a little, remembering the stuffed animal heads and skins I had seen in Aziz's study. "He kind of gives me the creeps."

"It seems so unfair to pull her away at the last minute like that! I wonder why Aziz didn't want her to come?" Julia asked.

We watched silently as Abla climbed into the limo, tears streaming down her face. She waved forlornly at us and then buried her face in her hands. Aziz was still outside the car, talking excitedly to Madame Bernoussi, the tour leader. He pointed at me, and whispered something. Madame Bernoussi looked at us and nodded.

"Am I crazy or does it look like they are talking about us?" I asked Julia.

"I don't know, Aili. I know you're crazy but I think you're right, they may be talking about us!"

We were still wondering about the strange events when the train whistle blew, announcing the final call to board the train for Marrakech.

"Come along girls!" Madame Bernoussi walked toward us. She was all smiles. "The Marrakech Express is about to leave! The other students are already all on board."

We quickly grabbed our backpacks and suitcases, jumped onto the train and were on our way to the Rose City!

Julia and I found two seats on the train facing each other and next to the window, with no one else in the two seats next to us. Our closest neighbors, two 7th graders, were across the aisle, next to the opposite window.

The train pulled away from the station and before long we were racing along the tracks bound for Marrakech. Julia and I put our backpacks on the empty seats next to us. I reached into mine, grabbed my Marrakech guidebook and immediately started to read. Julia had decided that she was going to keep a tape-recorded diary of her trip. The first thing she would report on was the strange behavior of Aziz at the train station, and on Abla's tearful departure. As she reached over to take the recorder from her backpack, Julia froze.

"It's moving!" she whispered to me, "My backpack is moving! There it goes again!"

Afraid to touch her bag, Julia watched, wide-eyed in disbelief as a small furry hand poked out from the bag.

"Maco!" she screamed. The other kids on the train turned and looked her way wondering what the commotion was about.

"Oh! Uh … I mean yeah, Maco!" Julia said looking around, trying to think of something to explain her outburst. She obviously didn't want the other students to know about the stowaway monkey. "Maco!! It's just a card game Aili and I are playing. She just got Maco so she lost! Too bad, Aili!"

I stared at Julia with a strange look on my face, but the other students just went back to what they were doing. Once things had settled down, Julia reached down and pulled out a startled but happy little Maco, both cheeks filled with raisins. He looked up at Julia knowing he had probably done something wrong. Julia put her jacket over the monkey to keep him hidden from view.

"Maco! He must have jumped into my backpack when we were at the train station!" Julia peeked under the jacket, "You crazy little monkey! What am I supposed to do with you now?"

10

Julia

The train to Marrakech sped along, stopping briefly at the port city of Casablanca to pick up more passengers. It then crossed through rolling farmland and pastures, and began making its way through the semi desert.

"You have to report the monkey, Julia," Aili whispered nervously looking around, "Abla will be frantic with worry!"

"I will, Aili!" I replied in a quiet voice, "But not now. Madame Bernoussi will just take him away from me. I can take care of Maco until we get to Marrakech. Then I'll call Abla and let her know we have him." I was not about to let Maco out of sight, let alone my arms.

Aili muttered under her breath, "This is crazy!" but went back to her reading leaving me to deal with the mischievous monkey.

For the first few hours, I managed to keep Maco pretty much of out of the way and out of sight, safely hidden in my large backpack. When the porter passed through the train selling drinks and snacks, I used some of my trip money to buy a bottle of water and a pack of peanuts. I got up to use the bathroom, clutching my backpack with my cute little stowaway and once safely in the locked bathroom, I let Maco out. He scampered around, investigating his surroundings. I tore open the bag of peanuts, and when he spotted the snack, Maco chattered excitedly and jumped onto my shoulders. Despite the strange situation, I couldn't help but smile at how cute and smart Maco was.

"Here you go, Maco!" I handed him some peanuts, which he promptly stuffed into his mouth. He chattered for more. "OK! OK! Now drink some water too!"

I helped Maco hold the bottle and he drank thirstily. While waiting for him to finish, I took out my tape recorder and started taping the rhythmic sound of the train clattering down the tracks. Looking out of the window, I saw that the train was approaching the Marrakech station.

"Time to get back in the backpack, Maco! We're here!"

I reached for the water bottle but before I could take it he screeched. I turned off the tape recorder.

"No, Maco!" I scolded him, "Give me the water bottle! We have to go!" This time I grabbed the bottle more forcibly and put Maco back into the backpack. I then quickly made my way back to our seats.

I saw Aili with her nose *still* in the guidebook. I knew she would now think she was an expert on Marrakech.

"I can't wait to see the High Atlas Mountains from Marrakech!" Aili began as she finally put down the book, "There is snow on them almost all year long! And," she continued enthusiastically as I settled back into my seat, "the *medina* of Marrakech is one of the largest living medieval cities in the world, and the Koutoubia mosque was built in the 12th century! That's 900 years ago!"

I fumbled with my backpack to make sure Maco would not be squashed. Aili was still going on about the sites of Marrakech when the train came to a stop.

"Aili put the book away! We're here! Let's go!"

The RAS student group got off the train and was herded onto an awaiting bus. The ride from the station to the hotel was quick, everyone eagerly looking out the windows at the magnificent city unfolding in front of them. Arriving at the Hotel Jardins de la Koutoubia, we were assigned rooms and told to meet in the lobby in 15 minutes. There were two chaperones per floor, but *Hamdullah,* not one in our room! I did a quick happy dance!

Once in our room, Aili started to unpack and I let Maco out of the backpack. The little monkey bounded around the room and stopped when he spotted a bowl of fruit, a welcoming gift from the hotel management. He was munching away on a banana when Aili asked, "Now what are you going to do with him?"

"Well, you saw how good he was on the train," I said hesitantly, "I could just keep him in my backpack until this afternoon. Anyway, we don't have time to call Abla now, we have to get downstairs!"

"Julia! Abla is going to be so worried!"

"Aili, it's already 10:30. We will be back at the hotel in a couple of hours for lunch and I'll call her then."

"I know what you are doing, Julia," Aili said, "If you call Abla now she'll tell you to give Maco to Madame Bernoussi. You just want to play with him some more. But he's not your pet!"

"You're right," I admitted. I then added "as usual" because I knew I could always soften Aili up by admitting she was right. "But just a couple of hours. Please Aili! I promise, never break a promise, I'll call at lunch and give Maco up. Please, please let me do this. I'll owe you," I pleaded, giving Aili my best puppy dog look.

"Yeah, you'll owe me, Julia. Big time." Then after a pause Aili added, "Fine. But just 'til lunch."

"You're the greatest, Aili!" I exclaimed, giving my sister a quick hug, "OK Maco! Into the backpack! Come on, let's go!"

Just to make sure he'd want to go in, I tossed in some dates and an apple from the fruit bowl into the backpack. Maco saw the treats going into the bag and got the idea. But being a greedy little monkey, he first grabbed two fists full of strawberries from the fruit bowl and then jumped into the backpack.

At the appointed time, we joined our classmates in the lobby. Madame Bernoussi began to speak.

"Welcome to Marrakech, boys and girls. You are going to have a wonderful adventure here. Marrakech is divided into two parts: the walled-in *medina*, or Old City, and the wide-open

New City called Gueliz. Gueliz is were the government offices are, and is less interesting, I think. The *medina*, however, is fabulous and mysterious."

She paused and looked at us. "Very mysterious," she said in a soft voice, "It is a living place. Finding your way can be confusing—you will see that the narrow streets and alleyways twist and turn, ending up in dead ends and blind corners. You must stay together in your groups, or you could get very lost! Here is a paper with the hotel address, phone number and my cell phone number too. Keep it with you in case you do get separated."

We were all assigned into groups of eight, each group with its own guide.

"Remember," Madame Bernoussi continued, "keep your guide in sight at all times. And when you hear *BALEK*! *BALEK*! move over! It means, "watch out!" probably because a donkey is coming through! All right, then. I will be at the hotel and will see you all at lunchtime. *Marhabam f' Marrakech*! Welcome to Marrakech!"

With that, the groups began to file out the lobby into the bright sunshine of Marrakech. Aili and I were happy about our group: besides us there were: two cute senior boys (Aili and I both thought that was great) two junior girls (that was less great) and two 6th graders (at least I was not the youngest in the group). After just a five-minute walk, we found ourselves at the Place Jema al Fna, the big square at the entrance to the *medina* of Marrakech. Even at eleven o'clock in the morning, the square was already filled with acrobats, dancers, cobra charmers, monkey tamers, fortunetellers, astrologers and even tooth pullers! Big wooden carts filled with oranges, tangerines and grapefruits were parked all over the place, squeezing fresh juice for anyone willing to pay the cost—one dirham (ten U.S. cents) per glass!

At the square, the groups separated and our group headed through one of the many *Babs* (gates) into the heart of the *medina*. *Medina* means city in Arabic, but in Morocco it is the name for the old walled quarters of a Moroccan town. The name comes from the city in Saudi Arabia where Mohammed, the founder of the religion of Islam, settled in the 7th century after he left his home in the city of Mecca. The Marrakech *medina* is an exotic, medieval town within a town, an intricate maze of alleyways, passages and streets. Our group shuffled along, passing first through the spice market, where merchant after merchant proudly displayed their wares in huge cone-shaped piles of orange, purple and brown spices, each more exotic than the other. The spices perfumed the air as we headed toward the *henna* market.

"What's *henna*?" I asked our group leader, whose name was Saida. I had heard of it before but wasn't exactly sure what it was. We had paused for a moment in front of a shop that displayed bags of a brown powdery substance.

"Henna is a type of dye that many Moroccan women use to color their hair to give it a reddish appearance," Saida explained, "And, if you mix this with water," she grabbed a handful of henna powder, "it becomes paint-like and is used to make tattoos on women's hands and feet."

"Tattoo!" I exclaimed. I had always thought it would be so cool to have a tattoo, just a little one, on my ankle. "I want to get one!"

Aili looked at me with a horrified expression. "You're crazy! Mom and Dad would kill you! Plus tattoos are dangerous!"

"Actually, Aili," Saida said, "the *henna* tattoos are not real tattoos. They are just temporary dyed tattoos. Have you noticed the hands and feet of some Moroccan women? They decorate themselves with flowery designs made from henna for special occasions, like weddings. They really are just drawings painted with an ink made from the *Henna* plant. When it dries, it looks reddish brown."

"I still want one!" I insisted.

"Well, maybe you can get one with your parents one day," Saida said, starting to walk away from the shop, "but not today. We have many more things to see!"

With that, our group explored deeper into the *medina* through the jumble of twisting lanes and small squares.

Saida continued with her explanations, "As you know, students, *Muslims* is the name given to people who believe in the religion of Islam. Like Christians believe in Christianity and Jews in Judaism."

"And Muslims pray to God in a Mosque," said Aili, "Like Christians pray in a Church."

"Like Jews pray in a Synagogue!" I added, not to be outdone by Aili.

"Correct, Aili and Julia!" Saida said, and then asked, "Does anyone know the name of the Holy Book of Islam?"

"You mean like the Christian Bible?" one of the 6th graders asked.

"Yes. Like the Bible or the Jewish Torah," Saida answered, "Do you know what it is called?"

One of the senior boys said. "It's called the *Koran*," and then smiled knowingly at the group, "Muslims believe that God gave the words of the *Koran* to Mohammed."

"Excellent." Saida smiled. Aili and I also smiled, and blushed a bit, both of us thinking how adorable the boy was.

But there was not much time to pay attention to the boy, because we wanted to discover the rest of the *medina* unfolding before us, an exotic, mysterious place. We passed beautiful fountains, elaborate palaces, and merchants selling just about everything, from leather slippers and intricately decorated mirrors and boxes, to shimmering silky cloth, richly woven carpets and magnificent, silver jewelry. The medina itself was made up of many small independent villages, each containing a mosque, a *hammam* (a public bath), a bakery, a fountain and a *medersa* (a school for studying the Koran). Every few minutes, I hid behind a stall and peeked inside my backpack to check on Maco. He had been curled in a ball, asleep, for most of the tour.

Almost everywhere in the *medina* we noticed cats stretching lazily in the warm sun, but not many dogs.

"I've hardly seen any dogs," I said, thinking of Bailey.

Saida explained, "That is because many Muslims consider them dirty. In fact, after they pet a dog, they must wash their hands seven times before they can go into a Mosque to pray."

Following the narrow lanes, our group soon found itself in front of the *medersa* Ali Ben Youssef.

"Over 900 students from various Muslim countries come to this *medersa* to study the *Koran*. It is very famous all over the Muslim world. Look over there. See that little building?" Saida was pointing to a small structure inside the Medersa, "That is a mosque, like a church or synagogue, where Muslims pray. It has a beautifully carved cedar-wood ceiling."

Since it was a Friday, all the doors to the mosque were opened. Although in most Arab countries, mosques are open to anyone, Aili and I knew that in Morocco, non-Muslims like us were not allowed to go in. So I stood to the side and I tried to peek through one of the open doors. But because all the other students were trying to do the same, I couldn't really get a good view. So instead, I walked around the corner, motioning for Aili to follow me. As we approached one of the mosque doors on the other side, we could hear loud voices coming from a corner café just a few feet away. A man was yelling at someone, yelling in English. Distracted, we turned to see what the commotion was about.

In the dim light of the café, I could just barely make out a man dressed in a brilliant white *jelleba* jabbing his finger toward a woman, with her back facing us, seated at one of the little tables. The man's voice was deep and menacing.

"I will say this in English so that no one else here will understand us. You will sign these papers. Now."

Aili and I had made our way to the side wall of the café, and listened as the man continued.

"That voice!" Aili whispered to me urgently, "I know that voice! You know that feeling you get when something is on the tip of your tongue but you can't think of what it is? That's what I'm feeling now and it's driving me CRAZY!"

The man continued, "Once these papers are signed we can ship out more of the animal skins and horns. We have to move quickly because our customers are waiting."

"Oh my gosh, Julia! I know who it is! Julia! It's Aziz! It's Abla's stepdad!"

I was already sort of afraid of Aziz, and to see him here in Marrakech, after the scene at the train station earlier today was a little frightening. Aili and I started to tiptoe away when I heard something that made me grab her arm and both of us turn around in shock.

"Ambassador Turner is a fool," Aziz was saying, "He does not see what is happening in his own Embassy. 'Save the Animals!' The Americans love to say that. Yet who will be blamed for allowing the export of the endangered cheetah skins and tortoise shells? The head American in Morocco! You have to admit, the irony is delicious." He laughed (in quite an evil way, I might add) at the thought of it.

I could not believe my ears. This man was plotting against our father! My heart was pounding and my palms were sweating horribly. And I suddenly realized that if we were seen, Aili and I would be in extreme danger.

"Sign these papers," Aziz demanded, "You are the only one who knows the Ambassador's signature." He pulled a pen out of his pocket and handed it to the woman at the table, "Sign them, and we will all be the richer, and no one will be the wiser."

The woman, whose back was to us, took the pen, and hesitated. As she lifted her hand from the paper, the stack of silver bangles on her right hand tinkled.

"When we will all become rich," Aziz laughed, fingering the woman's bangles, "you can replace these cheap bangles with diamond bracelets!"

A moment later, we heard the scraping of chairs against the floor. Aziz and the woman were getting up from the table!

"We have to get out of here *now!*" Aili hissed to me, her usually even voice shaking with fear, "before they see us! We have to warn Daddy!"

Aili grabbed my arm and spoke quickly and quietly, clearly trying not so scare me. It wasn't working. "Try to get back to the group, Julia! Go now!"

I hesitated, and Aili said more firmly, "Go, Julia! Don't stop and don't look back!"

By now the rest of the students in our group had already started to walk away from the mosque toward the next site. In the confusion of people coming and going in the narrow lanes, Saida, our tour leader, had not noticed that Aili and I were not with them.

I nodded fearfully and crept away from the café. When I thought I was clearly out of sight, I began to run. Aili was right behind me as we zigzagged through the maze of the *medina*. We ran past date sellers and spice merchants, past ladies dressed in caftans shopping for their noontime meal. We dodged a woman selling pigeons and narrowly missed knocking over a huge display of blue and white Fez pottery. As we rounded the bend of a narrow alleyway, a boy leading a donkey pulling a cart full of carpets crossed right in front of us. Trying to avoid colliding with the boy and his animal, I moved sharply to my left and crashed instead into an olive seller's stall.

"*Balek! Balek! La la la!*" the merchant shouted.

"*Smahlee*! I am so sorry!" I cried out and stopped to help him pick up the scattered olives.

Aili soon caught up to me and shouted, "Come on! We have to get out of here!"

"But I feel so bad leaving him like this!" I answered, quickly trying to gather up the olives, which were rolling around all over the street.

"Maybe I can help," a man said in English. He was standing right behind Aili and me. I whirled around and to my horror came face-to-face with a man, his jagged scar quite visible and more haunting than ever.

Aili's panicked voice rang out across the *medina*, "It's Scarface, Julia! Run! RUN!"

11

Aili

I watched Julia scramble to her feet and begin running down
the alley when I felt Scarface grab my shoulders. I screamed
and struggled to get out of his grip.

"Calm down! Quiet!" the man said, "I don't want to hurt
you!"

I continued to struggle, but soon realized that I wouldn't be
able to break away. The merchants and passersby in the *medina*
shook their heads, thinking that I was a naughty child being
scolded by my father. I knew they wouldn't help me. But at that
moment, rather than feeling sad or scared, I felt unexpectedly
angry.

This guy can't do this to me! I thought to myself, and I became
determined to do something about it. As we started walking
back in the direction of the café, his hand still tightly gripping

my shoulder, I could once again smell the pungent odors of cardamom, mint and paprika. We were passing back through the spice market. Coming alongside a great cone shaped pile of spicy cayenne pepper, I grabbed a handful, twirled around, and threw it into Scarface's eyes.

"Ayeee!" he cried as his hands released me and reached for his eyes. Temporarily blinded by the pepper, he could not see me as I turned around and raced to catch up with Julia.

The *medina*, which had seemed so exotic and exciting just a short while ago, now seemed like a maze in a nightmare. The narrow lanes twisted, turned and doubled back; the windowless houses all began to look alike, and, as clouds passed in front of the sun, an eerie darkness began to engulf the *medina*.

"I am so lost!" I moaned to myself, "How am I ever going to find Julia? She must be lost too!"

After fifteen minutes of running and darting about, I was exhausted. Nothing looked familiar anymore. With my blond hair and American clothes, I felt like I stuck out like a sore thumb. The men and women were all wearing traditional caftans, and some of the women were covered with *burkas* that hid their faces. The children playing soccer in the narrow alleyways eyed me warily as I walked around panting and dazed, looking up and down the streets, trying to find a way out.

"Do you speak English?" I asked a group of skinny boys kicking an old deflated ball in an alleyway. They stared at me and giggled, pointing fingers and saying something in Arabic I couldn't understand.

"*Shokran* anyway," I thanked them, mixing up my Arabic and English. I started to walk away when I heard a voice call to me.

"*Lalla! Lalla!* Come with me!" I turned and instantly recognized the young boy with his donkey, the same one who just a while ago had almost crashed into Julia.

"*Lalla!* I can help you!"

You've already done enough, I thought to myself, thinking that he was the reason Julia and I were now separated. I turned from him and started to walk away, "*La!* No! Just go away. I can ..."

The boy interrupted me, "I have your sister!"

I turned around like a shot. "What? What do you mean?"

"Yes, I saw what happened ... the man with scar ... catching you ... chasing her ... so I said to myself, Youssef, you must help. So I help. I hide her under carpets in donkey cart and took her to my home. She is safe and is awaiting you."

I felt nervous. I knew that I should never follow a stranger to a strange place, but this time I felt I didn't have a choice. The boy seemed to be telling the truth, and without him, I realized I didn't have a chance of finding Julia. But I was still scared.

"Do not be afraid," Youssef said, as if reading my mind, "Julia is waiting for you. She said to tell "Fat Face" to come with me".

For the first time in my life, I was overjoyed to hear my hated nickname and knew Youssef must be telling the truth.

"OK, thank you!" I said with an enormous sigh of relief, "Please take me to Julia!"

Youssef, the donkey and I made our way along the twisted streets and finally stopped in front of a door, richly carved and studded with brass nails. The door had two knockers: one, shaped like a person's hand, at eye level, and the other, a ring shaped knocker, above it, too high to reach, because it was used in the olden days when visitors arrived on horseback.

"Julia! Where are you?" I cried out as, following Youssef's lead, I took off my shoes and stepped across the threshold into the house. At that moment, a door opened across the courtyard and Julia came running out towards us.

"Aili! Aili!" Julia called out, "Are you ok? I have never been so happy to see you!" Julia squealed. I felt the exact same way.

"Julia!" we hugged, "I was so scared when I couldn't find you!"

"And I was so scared when that man grabbed you. I ran to try to get help and ran into Youssef. He said he knew the *medina* better than anyone, and would find you and bring you here. And he did!" Julia grinned towards him.

I turned to speak to the kind boy, "Oh Youssef, thank you for all your help. But we don't want to bother you anymore. We really should leave and get back to the hotel and tell Madame Bernoussi what happened."

"But first, you must eat," a woman's voice rang out from across the garden.

Julia and I turned around and saw an elegant woman in a flowing lavender caftan walking towards us.

"*Feed your guests even if you are starving* is famous Moroccan proverb," she continued in a heavy Moroccan accent.

"And my mother always follows it!" Youssef smiled, "I am afraid you do not have choice. My mother will be offended if you do not eat just a little something."

Julia and I looked at each other—we knew hospitality was extremely important to Moroccans and we also knew if we refused to eat we would be insulting the family. It would be terrible to offend the family who had saved us, but we obviously had to report what had happened to us.

Youssef saw that I looked worried. "Don't be concerned. Call the hotel and I will tell them where you are. They can come get you." Youssef took out his cell phone.

I dialed Madame Bernoussi's number and got her voicemail, which I thought was a little weird. I told her that we were safe and asked her to send someone to get us. I handed the phone to Youssef and he gave the address and instructions on how to get to the *riad*.

"While we wait," Youssef said, after he hung up the phone, "you must eat!"

Finally able to relax a bit, I took a look around the *riad*. The traditional Moroccan house, or *riad*, consists of rooms built around a courtyard, open to the sky. The ceilings are very high and the walls are enormously thick, keeping the *riads* cool in the summer and warm in the winter. Small windows look into the courtyard, but not into the *medina* street, so you feel you are in an oasis of calm when you enter a *riad*.

"Oh, this is so beautiful!" I exclaimed gazing at the lovely courtyard, filled with towering palm trees, fig trees, flowers and a burbling fountain in the middle. *Zeleej*, the Moroccan mosaic tiles in blue, green, red, yellow and white decorated the riad walls and floors. Youssef's mother told Julia and me about Moroccan design.

"All decoration in Morocco always geometric patterns, such as squares and star shapes, or floral designs. You never see decorations that show animal or human shapes."

When we looked a little confused, Youssef explained, "This is because in our religion, Islam, designs showing humans or animals are not allowed. I know in Christian churches you have many paintings and drawings of Jesus, the saints and others. In Islam we do not have such paintings."

"It feels so much cooler in here than outside on the street!" Julia remarked. It had been so hot in the streets of the *medina*, and running around in a frenzy hadn't helped. "Do you have air conditioning?"

"No," replied Youssef, "It is cool in here because the sun can only come in through that opening in the courtyard roof." He pointed to the fountain, "And the water also helps keep it cool. As do the plants."

"It's like an oasis in the middle of the *medina!*" I exclaimed.

"Please, sit here." Youssef's mother motioned us to a small, knee high table positioned in front of a low sofa piled with pillows. We did as she asked and settled down comfortably. Julia had just taken off her backpack and laid it on the floor when out popped Maco!

"Oh my gosh!" Julia cried out in surprise, "It's Maco!" She opened her arms and beckoned for him to come to her but the little monkey was clearly much more interested in the various plates of food and jumped straight from Julia's backpack to the edge of the table.

"*Willi, willi!*" Youssef's mother exclaimed, recoiling a bit.

"Oh! I am so sorry Madame!" Julia apologized as she quickly grabbed Maco before he could reach for any of the food, "I totally forgot I had my pet monkey with me!"

The "*MY*" pet monkey line did not escape me, and I gave Julia a glaring look.

Youssef's mother surprised us all when she laughed and said, "*Makain mooshkil,* Julia! He reminds me of my pet monkey when I was a young girl in Fez! It is wonderful!" She clapped he hands and looked up towards the kitchen. "Bouchra!" she called to one of the servants, "Please take this little fellow to the kitchen and give him some food!"

"Oh please, don't bother Madame! He can wait in my back-pack," Julia said.

"Well, he shall at least have a banana," Youssef's mother said, and plucked one out of the fruit bowl in the center of the table. Julia handed the banana to Maco, who settled back into her backpack, happy with his prize.

A moment later, the serving girl appeared with a kettle and a basin. Following Youssef's lead, I held my hands over the basin while the servant poured rose-scented water over them. A momentary horrified look crossed Youssef's mother's face when she saw how dirty Julia's and my hands were.

"Oh, my hands, no they're not very clean I'm afraid, what with the dates, donkey, dirt ... I am so sorry," Julia mumbled apologetically.

While we were waiting for the food to be served, I looked carefully at the tablecloth, or rather, tablecloths. Four of them, to be exact. Youssef noticed me looking and said, "Oh, the number of tablecloths tells you how many courses you will have. So when you go to a Moroccan's house for dinner, you'd better count the number of cloths so you can pace your eating! I have been to dinners where there were seven tablecloths!" Youssef laughed. "In Morocco, we serve a lot of food."

And this lunch was no exception. The first course was a spicy *Harira* soup made from lentils and served with lemon juice and dates. It smelled so good that I could hardly wait to dig in.

"*Bismillah,*" Youssef's mother smiled at us, "it means, "in the name of God" and we always say it before eating."

The soup was delicious. Full of flavor, but not too spicy.

"*Harira* is the first thing we eat during *Ramadan,*" said Youssef.

"Oh, *Ramadan!*" I remembered and looked up from my soup, "One of the five pillars of Islam that Abdu was going to tell us about! What is it, Youssef?"

"Well, *Ramadan* is the most important time of the year in any Islamic country," Youssef explained, "It commemorates the time in which the *Koran*, the Holy Book of Islam, was revealed by God to Mohammed. For one month we do not eat or drink anything from sunrise to sunset. This is called fasting. Not even a drop of water should pass a Muslim's throat."

Youssef's mother added, "Of course, if you are sick, or a child, or pregnant, you do not need to fast."

"And why don't you eat during the whole day?" I asked thinking there was no way I could ever go for five hours without eating, let alone an entire day!

"Because we Muslims need to feel what it is like to go without food and to say "no" to ourselves," Youssef said, "By not eating all day long, we can better understand people less fortunate than us who do not have all we have."

"It must be hard not to eat, but to not drink anything all day long ... I don't know if I could do it!" I said.

"Well, you get used to it," Youssef smiled, "And you feel good when you do it because it means something. And of course, there is always the *Iftar* to look forward to!"

Youssef's mother continued, "Every evening, after the sun sets and the call to prayer is heard, we break our fast, which means we eat. This is our *Iftar*. And the first thing we always eat is this exact soup, *Harira*."

"*Ramadan* lasts for about 30 days." Youssef added

The serving girls then took away the soup bowls and placed a large platter of couscous in the center of the table. No one was given an individual plate from which to eat. I watched carefully as Youssef's mother used her right hand to take some of the couscous from the part of the platter nearest her, roll it into a ball, and eat it delicately. Her left hand stayed in her lap. I knew that it was very rude to do anything, much less eat, with your left hand. In fact, in Arabic class at school I had been scolded by the teacher when I had handed in my assignment using my left hand. "*Lalla* Aili, the left hand is for personal hygiene only."

Julia and I followed our hosts' lead and neatly, or at least trying to be neat, ate the couscous with our hands. After the couscous, another dish was brought out.

"Ah! Now for the *pastilla!*" announced Youssef's mother proudly as she cut a large slice for Julia. Using her right hand, Julia took some and ate it. "This is really delicious, Madame," Julia smiled, "What is it again?"

"*Pastilla* is a favorite of ours—a flaky crust, and the meat flavored with almonds, saffron and cinnamon. They say the best *pastilla* is made in Fez, the city where I was born," Youssef's mother said proudly.

"Delicious!" Julia exclaimed as she munched on the *pastilla*.

Youssef chimed in, "Yes, delicious. And it is always so much more delicious when the meat you use is your own pigeons!"

My stomach flip-flopped as I pictured the birds we had seen in the market with our chef Abdu, and of the ones we had seen in the Marrakech *medina* earlier today.

"Oh!" I managed to say, my face turning pale, "your own pigeons." I took a big gulp of the sweet mint tea and felt a bit better. I had to admit the *pastilla* was pretty tasty, but I did not go for a second helping.

As we ate, I gazed around the room. Photos of the King and Royal Family were everywhere. I remembered Rashid telling me that the King of Morocco is a direct descendant of the Prophet

Mohammed. No one ever criticizes the King; in fact, insulting him is a criminal offense. King Mohammed VI, the current King, was a very popular king, Rashid said, and had made many reforms that helped the Moroccan people, especially women and children. His wife is a computer engineer!

Finally dessert was served: sweet pastries made out of almonds and an assortment of nuts and fruits.

"*Tangerines* come from the Moroccan city of Tanger, or Tangier as you call it," said Youssef proudly as he peeled one of the fruit. Funny, I had never thought of that!

After we finished dessert, Julia and I stood up, our bellies slightly protruding from the enormous lunch. "What a delicious meal. *Zween*! Thank you so much for inviting us!" I said to the mother, "*Shokran bezzef*."

"Oh you speak Arabic," she was delighted, "*La shokran alla wajeeb*, you are most welcome!"

As I popped one last sweet, ripe apricot in my mouth I heard a loud commotion at the front door.

"Where are the girls?" a shrill voice called out, "Out of my way! I demand to see the Ambassador's daughters!"

12

Julia

"There you are! You poor dears!" Madame Bernoussi bustled into the dining room, "What on earth happened? We have been worried sick about you two!" She surveyed the room in a haughty manner. "Did these people hurt you? Don't worry! I have brought security guards. They know how to deal with this type of situation." She signaled the two guards who then grabbed Youssef.

"These girls are the daughters of the U.S. Ambassador to Morocco!" Madame Bernoussi shouted, looking directly at Youssef, "You will pay dearly for harming them."

It all was happening so fast that we hardly had a chance to react.

"No!" Aili finally managed to cry out, "No! These people helped us! They didn't hurt us!"

One of the security guards was handcuffing Youssef.

"Let him go!" I shouted, "Stop it! He didn't hurt us! He was the one who called you and left the message!"

"Don't you worry anymore," Madame Bernoussi said, ignoring our pleas to let Youssef go, "We will take care of you and take you to your father. Come with us now!"

The guard held onto Youssef, while his mother tearfully begged him to let go of her boy.

Turning to Madame Bernoussi Aili cried, "Please let him go, Madame! He has done nothing wrong!"

A policeman had been called and arrived within a few minutes. The security guard handed over Youssef, and the policeman took him away. Youssef's mother followed behind, sobbing.

"Don't worry Youssef!" Aili called out after him. "We will explain everything and they will let you go!" She then turned to Madame Bernoussi and again said, "Please, Madame, let me explain!"

"I am so relieved to see you," Madame Bernoussi said over and over again, "Your parents are worried sick about you. Come with me, and I will take you to them right away."

"But Madame you have to help Youssef. He did nothing wrong," I pleaded, "In fact, he *saved* us."

"What are you talking about?" she demanded sharply.

Aili quickly explained the chain of events that had led us here. "Julia and I were being chased by a man with a scar, after we overheard Abla's stepdad talking to a woman and plotting with her," Aili said breathlessly, "And, and ... they are selling endangered animal parts!"

"And trying to blame our Dad!" I added.

"What? Who? Did you see whom he was talking to?" asked Madame Bernoussi, looking at Aili intently.

"No, but it was definitely a woman ... her back was turned to us, but I did notice ..." Just then, Aili and I heard a distinctive tinkling sound. Aili drew in a breath as Madame Bernoussi lifted her right hand to straighten her hair. On her wrist was a stack of silver bangles.

"Yes, dear? What did you notice?" asked Madame Bernoussi.

"I ... I ..." Aili stammered, "I ... um ... noticed that she had dark hair, but that's all." Aili turned to me, "Julia, put on your backpack and lets go get the rest of our things from the courtyard. I'll go with you." She turned to face me, sending a signal with her eyes to be quiet and just follow along. "We'll be right back, Madame."

Once outside in the courtyard, Aili spoke rapidly to me, "You saw the bangles on Madame Bernoussi's hand, right? SHE is the woman that was in the café with Abla's father! She is part of the plan to sell animals and blame Daddy! We have to get out of here now!"

Suddenly very afraid, I began looking around the courtyard to see if there was a way out. Aili did the same. Most of the old *riads* in the *medina* had only one entrance, and that was at the front of the house. But that was also where Madame Bernoussi was now waiting. How would we get out?

Panic was beginning to set in. Then, behind some small potted palm trees, I noticed a small arched door with a massive brass handle.

"I wonder where that goes?" I nudged Aili to make her look.

"Let's give it a try," answered Aili, already making her way towards the door. I followed quickly behind and when we approached it, we could hear the sounds of the street just outside. "This is a way out!" Aili almost shouted with joy. Together we placed our hands on the giant knob and tried to turn it. It wouldn't budge.

"It won't move!" Aili cried.

"Keep trying to turn it," I said, almost in tears.

Then I noticed a small keyhole just below the knob.

"It's locked!" I exclaimed, "We need the key. Look around and see if it is under a pot or something." I remembered that our mother always left a spare key under the potted geraniums at our house in Palo Alto.

"Is this what you are looking for?" The voice came from behind us. We spun around and saw Madame Bernoussi holding a small brass key. Her two security guards were with her.

"Yes, this looks like it would fit just exactly right," Madame Bernoussi said as she fingered the small key, "Let's give it a try, shall we?"

We shrank back in fear as Madame Bernoussi approached the door. She placed the key in the hole and turned it. The door creaked open, revealing the street and a black sedan parked in the narrow lane. "Get into the car," she snapped at us, "do it now, or my friendly guards will help you."

We both realized there was no way we could outrun two large security guards, exhausted and terrified as we were by the events of the day. So Aili and I got into the car and, afraid and shaken, held hands as the car sped away into the approaching evening.

"What do you want with us? Where are you taking us?" Aili finally managed to stammer.

"Do you think I am stupid, child? I know you realize I was the one in the café. How you figured that one out, I don't know." Madame Bernoussi ran her fingers through her hair and the bangles tinkled again. She looked at us menacingly, "Don't worry, if you cooperate, we will not harm you. We will let you go as soon as the job is done."

"Right," Aili whispered to me, "They will let us go as soon as the job is done and Daddy is blamed!"

13

Aili

*A*s the car made its way along the narrow streets of the *medina*, I tried to reason with Madame Bernoussi.

"Please, Madame, let us go. We won't tell anyone what we know."

"And just what do you think you know?" she demanded.

"Actually we don't know anything, really … I mean, I don't even know what the animal skins are and what they are used for …"

"Oh, an innocent. I suppose you are one of those people who cares about the poor tigers and rhinos. 'Oh, the poor elephant is dead and his tusks are gone'. 'Oh the tigers are being killed just for their skins, and soon there will be no more tigers.'" Madame Bernoussi laughed and shook her head, "Please. I have heard it all before. The animals are nothing, they don't have rights! If some fool is willing to pay me $5,000 for a tiger skin because he thinks it looks pretty on his floor, then I will make sure he gets it! If a man wants to drink powdered rhinoceros horns because he thinks it makes him stronger, than I will give him the horns, and he will give me a lot of money!"

She paused for a moment and then added, "And besides, if I don't do it, someone else will."

I could hardly believe my ears. I remembered photos I had seen of beautiful elephants, lying slaughtered on the jungle floor—killed just for their tusks. And of baby cheetahs, helpless because their mother had been killed so that a selfish person could cover his floor with her skin. It was too terrible. And to think that Madame Bernoussi could be so cruel and cold was frightening.

"And so you see," Madame Bernoussi continued, "I am only supplying people with what they want. People care too much about animals. I care about me."

Crossing through the Bab Ftouh, one of the fourteen gates leading out of the *medina*, the car entered the Place Jema Al Fna. The square was still crowded with jugglers, storytellers, and snake charmers. Horn blaring, the driver inched the sedan along while pedestrians weaved here and there, trying to avoid a collision. I thought about trying to jump out, but realized I would never be able to get away. As the car reached the end of the square it picked up speed and was soon racing down the road leading out of Marrakech.

"Where are we going? Where are you taking us?" Julia demanded.

"Somewhere safe. Now shut up. I don't want to hear your voices anymore. I need to take a nap. Nabil!" she barked at one of the guards, "Make sure the girls do nothing stupid while I rest."

"*Waha*," the man responded and gave us a stern look, "OK," he repeated in English, to make sure we understood him.

I looked glumly out the window. In the distance I could see the snow capped peaks of the High Atlas mountains and the rows of palm trees swaying in the breeze. The deep pink walls of Marrakech reflected the beautiful, warm light of the setting desert sun. But the warm beauty of the Rose City could not outweigh the cold fear growing inside of Julia and me as we wondered how our day would end. Within moments, a sign on the edge of the road confirmed to us that it was going to be a very long day indeed. "Casablanca—250 kilometers".

14

Julia

Of course both Aili and I knew about Casablanca. In fact, most people had heard of it because of the famous 1940s movie starring Humphrey Bogart and Ingrid Bergman. Some people even thought it was the capital of Morocco. "It's not the capital of the country," Dad had told us, "but it is the capital of the country's economy. It is in *Casa*, as the locals call it, that most of the big companies and banks are located."

I also remembered that Casa was also home to Morocco's biggest seaport. "Aili!" I nudged her, "I know where we are going! Casa has a huge port where ships from all over the world come to load and unload their goods. I'll bet that's where we're going."

By now, Madame Bernoussi had woken up from her nap and seemed to be even more cross than before.

"I just want to get this over with," she said to the driver in French, "I don't have a good feeling. The *"Princess"* sails at 4 AM. We have much to do and we need to hurry! Drive faster!"

"Oh my gosh, you're right, Julia!" Aili whispered, "We're going to the port of Casablanca! They are going to try to get the shipment of endangered animal skins out tomorrow morning!"

For the first time ever, I was grateful for Madame Raouf's French classes, and although I didn't say it to Aili, somehow just knowing *where* we were going made me feel better.

"We have to do something," I whispered back to Aili.

"I know!" replied Aili, "But what?"

The road from Marrakech to Casablanca is a good one, but traffic jams can be murderous. So, by the time we reached Casa, it was already almost midnight. We made our way through the still crazy city traffic and finally arrived at the port. Ships from many countries were tied up at the docks, and even at this late hour, there was a frenzy of activity as shipments were loaded and unloaded. The black car drove along the dock and finally stopped by two shipping containers marked "Algerian Orange Export Company". The containers were big metal boxes, about 40 feet long, and 8 feet high and wide, into which goods were packed. Once packed up, the container was lifted onto a ship, and the goods were transported to their final destination. A huge ship was tied up next to the containers. As Julia and I got out of the car we could see the name *"Algerian Princess"* painted on the ship's bow.

"This must be the ship they were talking about … the *"Princess"*, remember?" I whispered, recalling Madame Bernoussi's conversation with the driver. "They're going to use it to smuggle out the endangered animal skins and parts!"

Before Aili could answer, Madame Bernoussi grabbed both of us by our arms.

"Come along, girls. No screaming or crying out. It won't do you any good anyway. The men here work for me. They won't help you."

She pushed us roughly toward one of the shipping containers.

"We are only going to use one of the containers for the shipment, so I think this other one would be a very nice place to *contain* you for a few hours," said Madame Bernoussi in a cruel voice, smirking at her own pun.

"Please Madame, we won't tell anyone anything!" Aili said.

"That's right, you won't because you won't be able to. This shipment will soon be gone, and I will be gone with it." Madame Bernoussi forced Aili and me into the container through the loading door.

"It's useless to scream," she said watching us carefully, "I will leave the key in the outside of the door. In the morning, after the ship has sailed, the day watchman will make his patrol. He will let you out and you can run home to Daddy. But by then it will be too late. We will be gone and your father will be blamed, and no one will believe your story!"

With that, Madame Bernoussi slammed the loading door closed, and we could hear a lock turning on the other side.

I looked around. There were no windows in the container, but we noticed that the light from the lamppost on the dock was filtering in through a ventilation shaft in the ceiling. The opening was no bigger than a soccer ball, so there was no way we could squeeze out. At least we could see each other, but surrounded by four metal walls, and a metal ceiling, we were frightened and disheartened. We tried to open the door but, as we suspected, it was locked tight.

Slumping down, we sat on the floor sitting as close to each other as possible. We hugged tight.

"Wow, I can't believe this is really happening," Aili said, looking more fragile and scared than I have ever seen her. I looked at my watch: 12:30 AM.

I was trying my best to stay positive. At least we were still alive and out of harm's way—for now. I also knew I needed to stay strong for Aili, who was now shivering and letting out muffled sniffles. "We'll be ok, Aili," I cooed softly, "Everything's going to be fine." I began to realize the role-reversal going on as I rubbed Aili's shoulders; for the first time *I* began to feel like the older, wiser sister.

A little squeak jolted us and I quickly remembered Maco was still in my backpack. He had been so quiet for the hours we spent in the car, nobody seemed to have noticed him. "Come on out, little guy," I said encouragingly. Maco popped out and climbed sleepily into my lap. Sensing my sadness, he sat quietly, snuggling against my arm. *Sweet little monkey.*

Outside Mme Bernoussi was shouting orders to the dock-workers. "Faster! Everything must be loaded before the ship sails. We only have less than four hours left!"

It was both frustrating and depressing not to be able to do anything to stop what was going on. I sat stroking Maco, and watched as Aili drifted off to sleep. I stayed awake for a few more minutes trying to think of a way out … but I could not come up with a plan, and before long, I too fell asleep.

A few hours later, just a little before 4 AM according to my watch, Aili and I both awoke with a start when we heard loud voices outside the container. One of the voices sounded very familiar.

"What have you done with the Ambassador's daughters?" The voice belonged to Aziz! "They must not ruin our plans."

"Don't worry, Aziz, they are safely locked in that container," replied Madame Bernoussi.

"Let me see the papers again," Aziz's voice was low and serious.

Madame Bernoussi must have handed them to Aziz. "Ah, yes, perfect!" he remarked, "The permission to export these animal skins is signed by none other than Thomas T. Turner, the U.S. Ambassador!" Aziz laughed loudly.

"Signed by me, you mean!" snickered Madame Bernoussi.

"Yes, *forged* by you. And an excellent job. I only wish I could be in Rabat when the police accuse the Ambassador and the Embassy staff," Aziz paused and was likely enjoying the thought, "It will be so wonderful."

"Yes, sir," agreed Madame Bernoussi, "A perfect plan."

Inside the container, Aili and I looked at each other with horror.

"So it's true!" Aili whispered to me, "Aziz is the ringleader of the endangered animal smuggling!"

"And he is trying to make it look like Daddy was part of the plan." I was now more angry than frightened. "We need to get out!"

"Yeah, but we also need to have some proof that Aziz is involved. Right now all the evidence points to Daddy as being the smuggler. And no one is going to believe our word against Aziz's." Aili pondered the problem. "Proof, proof, proof … Pictures! Julia, do you have your camera with you?"

"Yeah, but that won't do us any good! There are no windows here so we can't get a shot of him."

"You're right ..." I could tell Aili's mind was racing as she emptied our backpacks onto the floor. "A pencil, a guidebook, gum, camera, tissues, pens ..." She sorted though the contents that had been spilled out.

We both saw it at the same time.

"The tape recorder!"

"We'll get him on tape!" I was ecstatic.

Quickly I punched the "record" button on the machine, and placed it as close to the edge of the door as possible.

"The shipment must go. There is no time to waste," Madame Bernoussi was saying.

Then Aziz's voice, "I know, that is why I am at the Port now. I could have let others do this part, but I want to be sure nothing goes wrong. I'll get back to Rabat once the shipment is on its way."

The conversation ended abruptly and I could just make out the sound of trucks moving along the docks, and the rumbling of motors and the clanking of chains. We listened for what seemed hours, and then it was all quiet. I switched off the recorder.

"Well, that's that," Aili said glumly, "I guess the shipment is going."

"We still need to get out of here!" I replied

"But there is no way out," Aili said, "We've checked everything."

Aili stared up at the ventilator shaft opening. "That's so small you'd have to be a weasel to wriggle of out that," she said, "I wish I had a weasel," she daydreamed out loud.

"Come back here!" My voice brought Aili back to the real world, "Maco! Come back!"

"Julia, what are you doing?" Aili asked.

"Maco just jumped out … he was napping in my backpack … or should I say in my *nap* sack!" I laughed feebly at my own joke.

"I don't know how you can make jokes at a time like this, Julia. We're in real trouble." Aili was annoyed.

Maco was scampering around the container, jumping up and down and generally acting like a monkey.

"Wait a minute! Maco!" Aili looked over toward the monkey, "Maybe Maco can squeeze through the ventilation opening!"

"Yeah, but then what? He'll just run away," I countered.

Aili sat and thought for a few minutes.

"Not if we train him!" she said, "You know he will do anything, I mean *anything* for food, right? So, we train him to bring the key to us!"

I thought it was certainly worth a try, and held out some raisins. "Come on Maco, come here!" I said. Obediently, the little monkey jumped into my arms and took the raisins from my hand.

In the meantime Aili was looking for something in the zipper section of her backpack. "Shoot! I don't have it. Julia, do you have your school locker key?"

I fished in my backpack and took out a key. I quickly got the idea.

"Here Maco! Look at the nice key!" I handed it to the monkey and he promptly put it in his mouth.

"No, Maco! Give me the key and I'll give you some more raisins." I held out the treat and Maco tried to grab some. But before he could, I took the key from his hand. Then he got his raisins.

"Let's do it again, Julia, so he learns that for a key, he gets raisins!"

I placed the key on the ground and said, "Get the key!" and held out the raisins. Maco kept going for the raisins, but ignored the key. Finally, by about the fifth time, Maco ambled over to the key, picked it up, handed it to me and greedily accepted the reward.

"What a smart monkey!" I cried out happily.

"Do it a few more time, Julia, so he definitely knows to associate the key with food."

Maco was pretty quick to get the idea. After a while, I placed the key by the door and Maco grabbed it and handed it to me. A few more times, and I thought he was ready for the real thing.

"OK, let's give it a try!" I said hopefully as I lifted Maco up to the ventilation opening; the monkey quickly grabbed a hold of the edge.

"OK, Maco! Good boy!" I said, "Do you want more raisins? Get me a key! Good boy!"

Maco just stared at me and then at Aili. Hanging from the opening by one arm, he seemed to have no idea of what we wanted.

"Oh no," Aili said gloomily.

"Maco! Good boy!" I held up the raisins, "Want more? Get the key!" I cried again, waving my locker key in the air. Maco grabbed for the key but I pulled my hand away.

"Not this key," I walked to the metal door, "over here! Outside the door, over here!" I banged on the door again and the monkey looked blankly at me.

"Julia this is not going to work. He ..." But before Aili could finish her sentence, the little monkey had squeezed through he grill and up through the ventilation shaft.

"He's out!" I cried, standing by the door, "Good boy Maco! Over here!" I banged again on the door near the keyhole, hoping Maco would go to the noise. I banged on the door for a while.

We waited for what seemed like ages.

Then, we heard a low clinking noise at the door. And then ... the sound of a key sliding out of keyhole! "He's got it! He's got it!" I cried out happily.

A few seconds later, Maco was at the ventilation opening, squeezing back through. He jumped into my open arms.

"Oh! Good boy! Here are your raisins, Maco! Good boy!" Maco chattered and squeaked as he handed me the key and grabbed his prize.

With Maco happily munching away, Aili and I devised a plan to warn our father.

15

Aili

*A*lthough we had not heard any voices since Madame Bernoussi and Aziz had left, we were still worried that there might be some guards outside near the container. We slid the key into the keyhole but before unlocking the door, pressed our ears against it, listening carefully.

"I don't hear anything," I said carefully, "I think they're all gone. Ok, let's go ..." and with that, I turned the key and opened the door.

It was still dark outside, but the dock was well lit. There seemed to be no one around. The big ship, "*Algerian Princess*", had left its berth. The other container with the endangered animal skins was gone, too.

"We don't have any time to lose!" I exclaimed to Julia, "Let's find a phone and call the Embassy."

Walking quickly, we soon exited the port area and found ourselves in the heart of downtown Casablanca.

"There's a taxi stand, Aili! Let's grab one!" Julia pointed to a long line of red cars.

"Those are *petits taxis*, Julia. They only take people inside the city limits of Casablanca. We need to go to Rabat, so we need a *grand taxi*," I sighed.

The *grands taxis* went from town to town and were usually shared by up to six passengers. Across from the line of *petits taxis*, I spotted what looked like a large parking lot of old white Mercedes, the *grands taxis*. The cars weren't in the best of shape—most of them dented, bashed and definitely well traveled. Running over to one of the drivers, I said, "*Combien pour Rabat*, How much to go to Rabat?"

"400 dirhams," the driver answered.

"*On y va*, let's go," I said and we jumped into the cab.

Once on our way to Rabat, I asked the driver if he had a cell phone.

"May I use it?" I asked and handed him a 10-dirham coin.

The driver nodded yes and passed me the phone. Dialing the embassy phone number, I was so relieved to hear the American voice on the other end.

"Marine Post 1, Sergeant Nahas." Came the familiar voice.

"Hi Sergeant! It's Aili Turner!" I cried, my voice shrill and excited.

"Are you alright? Where are you? Everyone is looking for you and is so worried! Is Julia with you? Are you ok?" he repeated.

"Yes, yes, we're ok," I assured him, "We're in Casa."

"We'll send a Marine van for you right away."

"No, its ok, we're in a *grand taxi* on our way home now."

"Are you sure you're ok?" the Marine asked again.

"Yes, yes, we're fine, I promise. Please connect us to our father."

"I'll patch your right through. The caller ID is showing me the cell phone number you are calling from—whose is it?"

"The taxi driver let me use it," I answered quickly, eager to connect with Dad.

"Ok, I'm patching you though to the Ambassador, and I'll check out the number you're calling from."

"Daddy! It's Aili and Julia!" I was almost crying as I spoke.

"Oh, girls! Oh my God! Are you ok? Where are you?" My Dad cried into the phone; I had never heard him sound so worked up.

"In a taxi, on the way from Casa to Rabat," I said and promised we would tell him everything when we arrived back at home.

"I am coming with two police cars to pick you up. Let me talk to the driver. I will tell him to keep driving toward Rabat and we will meet you at the Skhirat city turn off," Dad sounded very worried, "Please be careful, girls. Your mother and I love you both very much."

I gave the driver the phone and Dad gave him instructions. The driver then handed the phone back to me.

"Keep talking to me, Aili," Dad continued, "I want to keep this line open until we make sure the taxi driver is OK. The Regional Security Officer and Wayne Plant set up a command center at the Embassy after we found out you were missing. It's been crazy here, and your mother and I have been frantic with worry."

I told Dad I was so sorry to cause all the trouble, but in a weird way, knowing that the RSO and DCM had all been looking for us somehow made me feel safer. A few seconds later, a call from Sgt. Nahas to the Ambassador broke into our phone line.

"The taxi driver checks out, Sir."

Relieved, Dad said to me, "Ok, Honey. The driver is a good man. Let me talk to him again."

This time Dad told the driver that he was the U.S. Ambassador and would be arriving in Skhirat with two police cars in addition to his normal ten bodyguards.

"*Fhemtee?*" Dad asked if he understood.

"*Fhemt. Makain Mooshkil,*" came the answer from a now very nervous taxi driver.

16

Julia

*H*alf an hour later, we were with Dad and on our way to the Embassy. The ride was extra fast because of the police escort.

Aili and I explained everything to him in detail: the café, the endangered animals, the forged agreement and the roles of Aziz and Madame Bernoussi.

"Of course I believe you, girls," Dad said when we finished, "It's just that it sounds so unlikely. And I can't accuse an important business man of such a terrible crime without any proof."

"Daddy," I said, excitedly reaching inside my backpack, "we do have proof!" I pulled out my tape recorder, "Here it is! Right here!"

"What do you mean?" Dad asked.

"We taped Aziz while he was at the port making sure the shipment got out."

"Let's hear it," Dad said, his face grim.

I pushed the rewind and then the play button. He heard a loud screeching sound coming from the tape.

"What was that?" Dad looked at me and I quickly pushed the pause button on the recorder.

"Oh yeah, that was Maco. I had just shown him a bag of raisins."

"Maco? Who's Maco? And why does he care so much about raisins?"

I reached into my backpack and pulled out the little monkey. "This is Maco!"

Dad was completely taken aback.

"A monkey, Julia? How ever did you end up with a monkey?"

I told him the story quickly and ended with, "So you see, Dad, I'm completely responsible and know how to take care of a monkey. So don't you think I should be ..."

Dad cut me short, "Julia, please! Not now! Let's listen to that tape."

I pushed the play button again:

"The shipment must go. There is no time to waste."

"I know, that is why I am at the Port now. I could have let others do this part, but I want to be sure nothing goes wrong. I'll get back to Rabat once the shipment is on its way."

When the tape ended, Dad reacted immediately. He fished his cell phone from his pocket and started dialing. As he was doing so, Aili leaned towards me and whispered quietly in my ear, "Julia," she said, "you're a hero. You saved Dad with that recording. I'm so proud of you." Suddenly all the terror and apprehension I had felt over the last 24 hours washed away. My sister was proud of me. Really proud of me. I looked up at her.

"Thank you, Aili. I love you." I squeezed her hand. This was the best feeling in the world.

Much to our utter shock, Dad's first phone call was to none other than Aziz himself.

"Hello Aziz," Dad began as Aili and I exchanged fearful glances, "Yes, it's Ambassador Turner. Forgive me for calling you so early in the morning, but this is an urgent matter. Would you be able to come to my office? In about an hour? That is very kind of you. I am sorry for any inconvenience." Dad hung up the phone, "We are going to get to the bottom of this, girls. I'm so proud of both of you."

Again, I felt a rush of happiness and pride wash over me.

The Police Commissaire was already at the Embassy when Dad, Aili and I arrived. Aziz showed up a few minutes later. Once everyone was seated in his office, Dad began.

"Commissaire Mustapha and Aziz, thank you both for coming. This is very awkward so I will just get to the point as clearly as I can." Dad went on and explained in detail our entire story. He left out, however, the fact that he had a tape recording. I carefully watched Aziz's face as Daddy described the events of the day. He sat perfectly straight-faced. Dad concluded his account by adding, "Aziz, we have reason to believe that you are involved in all of this. In fact, we believe you are the mastermind of the smuggling ring. I am sorry."

Aziz just shook his head and smiled.

"Mr. Ambassador. It is *I* who am sorry. I was hoping I would not be forced to show this to the police. But, with your wild accusations, you have left me no other choice."

Turning to Commissaire Mustapha he pulled out some documents from his briefcase. "I was given these papers yesterday. I have long feared that there was some illegal export of precious endangered animal skins and parts. I have had an investigator looking into this problem. You can imagine my shock today when he came to me with these." He handed the documents to the Police Commissaire

"This is a shipping permit for a cargo of oranges which left today," said the Commissaire.

"Yes, oranges," Aziz smiled, "Please note the name of the ship."

"Let me see ..." The Commissaire scanned the page, "Ah! The *Algerian Princess*! Why, that was the ship that was seized about an hour ago off the coast of Casablanca! We had a tip that the cargo was not oranges! It was cheetah skins, rhinoceros horns and the like. All from endangered animals."

"Exactly, Commissaire." Then Aziz continued, "And now, please, see who signed the shipping permit."

The Commissaire's eyes went to the bottom of the page. "Thomas T. Turner."

"Yes, Commissaire. Thomas T. Turner, the Ambassador of the United States of America to the Kingdom of Morocco. *He* is the mastermind of the endangered animals crimes."

I couldn't take it anymore.

"No! Commissaire Mustapha, please! That is all a lie. We saw the woman who forged our father's signature, Madame Bernoussi. And we know she works for Mr. Aziz. They were together early this morning at the Port, just before the *Algerian Princess* sailed. They locked us in a container!"

"Nonsense, Commissaire," Aziz broke in, "I was at home fast asleep at that time. The *Algerian Princess* sailed at 4:00 AM!"

"But I can prove it!" I protested.

The Commissaire turned to me with a questioning look.

"Here," I pulled out the taper recorder, "Listen!" I switched on the machine.

"The shipment must go. There is no time to waste."

"I know, that is why I am at the Port now. I could have let others do this part, but I want to be sure nothing goes wrong. I'll get back to Rabat once the shipment is on its way."

The Commissaire now turned to Aziz. "You said you were not at the port. Yet your voice on this tape says you were there."

"Well, of course I was at the port yesterday. But that was in the afternoon. I was getting my shipment of clothing ready to go."

"So you were *not* at the port this morning when the *Algerian Princess* sailed?"

"I have already said no!" Aziz was getting angrier by the minute. "That tape proves nothing except that I was at the port. And as I have already said I was at the port yesterday afternoon."

The Police Commissaire made a quick call on his cell phone. In a few minutes he said, "We had a man check and you were indeed at the port yesterday afternoon. You are telling the truth. I am sorry to have accused you, Aziz."

"But this recording was made this morning! I promise you!" Aili exclaimed.

"HA! The fertile imaginations of two little girls who ran away from their tour group. They invented this whole crazy story so as not to get in trouble," Aziz glared at us cruelly.

"That's not true!" I protested.

"And they are trying to blame me to take away the blame from their father, the true criminal. Pitiful really, how children invent things."

Aili and I looked at each other, shocked at Aziz's lies. Then I said, "Please. Can we listen to the tape? One more time, please?"

I reached for my recorder.

"We already heard that, Julia," Dad said gently.

"Enough of this nonsense," Aziz demanded, "Commissaire, you must detain the Ambassador."

"No! Please just listen again … *closely*," I repeated, "Listen to what is in the background."

I rewound the tape and turned up the volume. The group listened to the recording once more. This time, ever so faintly, you could hear a man's voice in the background calling out "*Allah Akbar! Allah Akbar!*" followed by more words in Arabic.

"Do you hear it?" I said excitedly. The Police Commissaire nodded.

"It is the call to prayer," the Commissaire explained. "The muezzin, standing at the top of a minaret at a mosque calls all Muslims to prayer."

"Yes," countered Aziz, "but we Muslims are called to pray five times a day as you know. At dawn, at noon, in the afternoon, at sunset and at night. As I have said twice already, I admit to being at the Casablanca port but it was yesterday afternoon, at the time of the *afternoon* prayer." He looked around the room in a smug, satisfied way.

I was completely depressed. My plan had not worked—Aziz had outsmarted me with his reasonable explanation for the call to prayer on the tape. I had all but given up hope that we could prove our story when I noticed Aili's expression. She looked … happy! Then I turned to the Commissaire who was beginning to speak.

"Aziz. You are under arrest," he said as he grabbed the pair of handcuffs hanging from his belt and started walking towards Aziz.

"What? What do you mean?" Aziz was confused.

"You have told us three times that you were not at the Casa port this morning."

"That is correct," Aziz said.

"But it is not correct," countered the Commissaire. He saw Aili smiling and nodding her head, "Miss Turner? Would you like to clarify for Mr. Aziz?"

"Yes, thank you, Commissaire," Aili replied, "All the calls to prayer are all the same, morning noon and night. They all begin with *"Allah Akbar"*, "God is Great". But only the first call to prayer in the morning has a little something extra. The muezzin tells people *that it is better to pray than to sleep.* If you listen carefully, that is exactly what he is saying on this tape. This call to prayer on this tape is the *morning* call to prayer. And it proves you were at the port this *morning.*" Aili beamed at Dad and me.

"Exactly! Such excellent detective work, Miss Turner! Aziz Ahmed, you are under arrest for the sale of endangered animal skins, for forgery and conspiracy."

The Commissaire stood up and motioned to the policeman waiting in the other room. "Captain, escort Mr. Ahmed to the car and take him to the police station for further questioning."

Aziz scowled at us as he was taken away, "You interfering little brats. My plan was perfect! Perfect!"

"Not perfect enough," replied the Commissaire, smiling at Aili and me.

I looked up at my big sister, "Aili, *you're* the hero! I am so proud of *you!*" This time she grabbed my hand and we smiled at each other.

A commotion at the door to the Ambassador's office stopped all conversation.

"Let me pass!" a man was shouting at the Marine stationed outside, "I must see the Ambassador!"

Dad walked over to the door and motioned for the Marine to let the man pass.

I drew in my breath sharply. It was Scarface! Here in Dad's office!

"Daddy! Daddy!" Aili and I ran to our father.

"He's the one that tried to catch us in the Marrakech *medina*! He's part of the smugglers!" Aili cried out.

The man with the scar stepped into the room, his mouth tightly closed and his black eyes gleaming. He raised his arms and moved even closer to Dad.

"Daddy! Watch out!" we screamed.

I watched in horror and then in amazement as the man hugged Dad and then shook his hand.

"Girls, this is Colonel Otman of the Moroccan DGST, sort of like our FBI. He has been working with me on breaking up this ring of smugglers. He has been undercover, and was able to infiltrate the gang to try to find out their plans. It's thanks to Colonel Otman that the *Algerian Princess* was seized this morning by the Moroccan navy."

"But he tried to kidnap us in the *medina*!" Aili exclaimed.

"Oh no, *Lalla*!" said Colonel Otman, "Your father asked me to keep an eye on you girls after he told me you had seen me at Abla's house. He was afraid you had stumbled upon something dangerous, as you had! We didn't think you'd be comfortable knowing someone was following you around all the time, so we decided that I should be undercover. But I can certainly see that you take care of yourself, because I sure got an *eyeful* in Marrakech!" he added wistfully, rubbing his eyes.

Aili was mortified, "I am so sorry! I had no idea!"

"*Makain Mooshkil.*" The colonel answered, "You two girls have done an excellent service for Morocco and for the world's fight against the killing of endangered animals and the export of their skins and horns."

"What about Youssef?" Aili asked suddenly, remembering the terrible scene when the boy was taken away, "We have to help him! He is stuck in Marrakech in a jail somewhere. He had nothing to do ..."

"He is fine," interrupted Colonel Otman, "My men saw to his release early this morning. He is with his mother now and told us to be sure to say hello to Julia and ... and ...," he searched in his pocket for a piece of paper where he had written his notes, "and to *Fat Face.*" He looked at us quizzically.

Aili blushed and I started laughing. Dad walked over and hugged us both tightly, "I am so proud of you, girls!"

I smiled, "Well, Daddy, remember. We didn't do it alone." As I spoke, Maco popped his head out of the backpack. "The *real* hero, Sidi Maco!

Epilogue

A few weeks after Aziz's arrest, Aili and Julia were talking with Abla at the Rabat American School. It was the last day of the school year, and the girls were saying their goodbyes.

"Isn't it funny how things work out," Abla said, "When my mother heard about Aziz's arrest, she moved right back to Rabat. We never knew anything about the smuggling. It is just so horrible—that room! Aziz had forbidden me to go in it, and I was so scared of him, I never even tried to go in. That part is all so awful, but it is so great living with my mother again."

"But now you are leaving Morocco!" Aili said sadly.

"Yes, we are moving to Bangkok, the capital of Thailand."

"What about Maco?" Julia asked, "Is he going with you?" She was secretly hoping that Maco would have to stay in Morocco and that she could take care of him.

"Oh, he's going with us, of course. I would never leave him behind."

Julia tried to smile and say, "Of course!" but the disappointed look in her eyes gave her true feelings away.

"Well, you will just have to visit us, Julia!" Abla said brightly, "You have the whole summer to plan a trip! You both could come and stay with us. We can go to the beach, shopping, visit temples and see wonderful sites! What do you think?"

Aili and Julia looked at each other. The mysterious East … the land of silks and spices … elephants and temples … *HAMDULLAH* and *HAIT!*

Join Aili and Julia on their next adventure in Thailand. Look for "BANGKOK SURPRISE" coming soon online and to your local bookstore. But before you go, visit <u>www. thepassportseries.com</u> and enter code "maco" to get your own diplomatic passport and the stamp for "Moroccan Mystery"!

Moroccan Arabic!

*These are some of the words used in **Moroccan Mystery**. How many can you remember?*

Afek - please
Allah - God
Allah Akbar – God is Great
Bab – a gate or door
Baboosh – soft leather slippers
Balek – watch out!
Bekhair - Fine
Bismillah – in the name of God
Caftan – A Moroccan Dress
Couscous – a North African dish made from wheat
Dada – similar to a nanny
Dirhams – the money in Morocco
Fhemtee? / Fhemt – do you understand? / I understand
Haj – the pilgrimage to Mecca
Hamdullah – Praise God
Hammam – a bath
Hanoot – a small shop
Hijab – A scarf worn around the head
Iftar - breakfast
Islam – the religion of the Muslim people, founded by Mohamed
Jelleba – white robe/dress worn by men

Jooj – two in Moroccan Arabic
La - no
La shokran alla wajeeb – no thank you
Labess – how are you
Lalla – the polite form of address for a lady
Makain mooshkil – no problem
Marhaba - welcome
Mecca – a city of Saudi Arabia, the center of Islam
Medersa – a school
Medina – City
Pastilla – a Moroccan dish of flaky pastry and meat
Riad – an old house
Salaam wa alaykum – a greeting, literally "Peace be with you"
Shokran – Thank you
Shokran bezzef- thank you very much
Si, Sidi – a polite way of addressing men
Smahlee – excuse me
Waha - ok
Zeleej – the beautiful mosaic tile work
Zween – beautiful or good

MOROCCAN MYSTERY CROSSWORD

Try your luck with Moroccan Arabic!
(Answers on next page)

Across
1 do you understand
5 mosaic tile
8 in the name of God
11 welcome
12 breakfast
13 small shop
16 North African dish made
from wheat
17 Moroccan dress
18 ok
19 the money of Morocco
22 no
25 how are you
27 hello
28 scarf worn over the head

Down
2 no problem
3 school
4 thank you
6 polite form of address for a
man
7 flaky pastry and meat pie
9 soft leather slippers
10 bath
14 old house
15 door or gate
20 city
21 good or beautiful
23 please
24 polite form of address for a
lady
26 God

MOROCCAN MYSTERY CROSSWORD

Answers

Across

1	do you understand
5	mosaic tile
8	in the name of God
11	welcome
12	breakfast
13	small shop
16	North African dish made from wheat
17	Moroccan dress
18	ok
19	the money of Morocco
22	no
25	how are you
27	hello
28	scarf worn over the head

Down

2	no problem
3	school
4	thank you
6	polite form of address for a man
7	flaky pastry and meat pie
9	soft leather slippers
10	bath
14	old house
15	door or gate
20	city
21	good or beautiful
23	please
24	polite form of address for a lady
26	God

THE PASSPORT SERIES

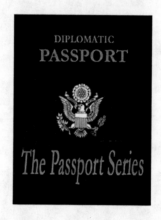

A passport to cultural adventures for middle readers

978-0-595-48696-0
0-595-48696-7